A Giant Problem

ALSO BY TAE KELLER

The Science of Breakable Things
When You Trap a Tiger
Jennifer Chan Is Not Alone
Mihi Ever After

TAE KELLER

Illustrated by
GERALDINE RODRÍGUEZ

A Giant Problem

HENRY HOLT AND COMPANY
New York

Henry Holt and Company, *Publishers since 1866*
Henry Holt® is a registered trademark of Macmillan Publishing Group, LLC
120 Broadway, New York, NY 10271 • mackids.com

Our books may be purchased in bulk for promotional, educational, or business
use. Please contact your local bookseller or the Macmillan Corporate and
Premium Sales Department at (800) 221-7945 ext. 5442 or by email at
MacmillanSpecialMarkets@macmillan.com.

Library of Congress Cataloging-in-Publication Data is available.

First edition, 2023
Book design by Aurora Parlagreco
Printed in United States of America by Lakeside Book Company,
Harrisonburg, Virginia

ISBN 978-1-250-81422-7
1 3 5 7 9 10 8 6 4 2

✥ **Chapter 1** ✥

ihi Whan Park was sitting in the library for indoor recess.

Again.

Two months ago, she'd:

1) discovered a portal to a fairy-tale world
2) met Sleeping Beauty, Snow White's evil queen, and Goldilocks's three bears
3) survived a horde of enchanted ladies-in-waiting.

You'd think after all that her life would have fundamentally changed. But instead, here she was again. In trouble.

Or maybe it was more accurate to say things *had* changed—and that was exactly the problem.

After spending time in the Rainbow Realm, Mihi's perspective on her own world had shifted. She'd always taken certain things for granted: She wasn't great at school. She wasn't popular. Her parents' pet shelter was always facing varying degrees of money problems, despite their hard work.

Before, those things had seemed entirely unchangeable.

But now . . . *fairy tales were real*. She could step through a refrigerator, right into them. So how could she accept anything as a fact of life when the most fundamental facts (i.e., refrigerators are not portals) had been proven wrong?

Mihi looked down at the stack of envelopes in front of her.

As part of indoor recess punishment, her kind-eyed librarian had tasked her with stuffing envelopes with book order forms. It wasn't so bad really. And Mihi liked Ms. Lavender, so she didn't mind doing it.

"I shouldn't even be here," Genevieve Donnelly pouted. She flicked her blonde ponytail, which she'd tied up with a thin green ribbon.

Right. The worst part of today's indoor recess: Mihi had to endure Genevieve, formerly known as Mihi's best friend. Currently known as Mihi's arch-nemesis.

Mihi closed her eyes and breathed deeply. This was a trick her dad had taught her. *You're so reckless, darling Mihi,* he said. *Before you speak or act, close your eyes and take three deep breaths. Then use your words—thoughtfully.*

Inhale. Exhale.

Inhale. Exhale.

Inhale—

"Like, this is *your* fault," Genevieve continued. "This is *so* unfair."

"Yeah. It *is* unfair." Mihi exhaled.

For the record, it was *not* Mihi's fault. The girls still sat next to each other in class, and what had started

as a whisper-fight had escalated to a not-so-whispered fight . . . and then became indoor recess.

"Oh, please, Mihi." Genevieve sighed. "How do you expect to survive and thrive when you're living in a fantasy world?"

Of course. *Survive and thrive*. Genevieve's dad hosted a popular motivational podcast, and that was his motto: Don't just survive . . . *thrive!* At dinners with the Donnellys, Mihi had always felt less than, like she was doing something wrong, but she didn't know what the right thing was.

Now those feelings crept back. Which was totally bogus. "Genevieve, I'm strong enough to survive this world *and* a fantasy world—which you never could, by the way."

Genevieve scrunched her nose. "Weird, Mihi."

They went back to writing *Book Orders!* on the envelopes. Genevieve's handwriting was cheery, bubbly, and perfectly even. Mihi's always tilted up, like her words were reaching higher. She tried to write in a straight line, and failed.

Genevieve glanced at Mihi. "And I could thrive in *any* world, thank you very much."

Mihi's dad had given her some very good advice on how to control her emotions, but she could not for the life of her remember what it was. "Wanna bet?"

Genevieve didn't bother responding.

And Mihi felt that familiar crunch of shame, the one she always got when Genevieve ignored her. The fiery urge to bite back and get Genevieve's attention burned inside her. But then she thought of her new friends, Reese and Savannah. Thoughtful and resourceful, gentle and kind, they had a deep *goodness* that reminded Mihi to be better.

She inhaled-exhaled. Three times.

Then she turned to Genevieve . . . and noticed something.

Genevieve's shoulders hunched. Her right foot tapped. She blinked just a little too quickly.

Somebody else probably wouldn't pick up on it, but Mihi had been Genevieve's best friend for years. That kind of connection didn't disappear overnight. And Mihi knew: Her former friend was close to tears.

Part of Mihi was still angry. Part of her still wanted a fight. But instead, she asked, "Is everything okay?"

Genevieve sniffed. Blinked faster.

More than anything else, Genevieve hated crying. Nobody *liked* crying, of course. But Mihi figured crying was a part of life, like traffic before school, or rainy days, or the fact that even though each new puppy at the pet shelter would inevitably pee on her, she knew she'd fall head over heels in love with them anyway.

During their friendship, whenever Genevieve got close to tears, Mihi felt like it was her job to make her friend happier. And she'd always done that by distracting her with a fantastical story.

"Hey, wanna hear something cool?"

Genevieve glanced at Mihi, her eyes almost hopeful.

Mihi plowed on. "Once upon a time, there was a girl. Like, a really cool, brave girl. And she and her friends found a portal into a magical world. All they had to do was eat one of Ms. Lav—Ms. . . . Lilac's magical candies, and a doorway appeared in the library refrigerator. They stepped through and met princesses and witches and a really terrifying woman named Bertha. She turned into a zombie for a moment, but honestly, she was scarier as her true self."

Genevieve half laughed, but not in a mean way. She sniffed, and her shoulders relaxed, and her eyes said, *Thank you.*

Mihi remembered now: Genevieve could make her feel really bad—but Genevieve could also make her feel really special.

"Where do you come up with this stuff?"

Mihi hesitated, then told the truth. "Sometimes I think I want fairy tales to be real so badly that I actually make them happen."

Genevieve half smiled, but sadness flickered beneath her expression.

"Is everything okay?" Mihi asked again, quieter this time.

Genevieve bit her lip. She tapped her pen on the table. *Tap, tap, tap.* And Mihi thought maybe they could go back. Maybe she could forget that Genevieve called her *weird* and *annoying,* and that the words had caused a terrible rip—something that had been fraying for a while until it finally happened, a tear in their friendship that felt impossible to mend.

What if Mihi could befriend Genevieve again?

Would it be different this time? Would Genevieve get along with Reese and Savannah?

But then Genevieve's jaw hardened, and she stood up. "I'm too old for made-up stories," she said, grabbing her backpack. "I'm not like you."

"Oh." Mihi felt the pain of Genevieve's disdain all over again. It was simultaneously sharp and numbing, like the cold-burn of winter on gloveless hands.

"I'm going to go do this at the front of the library," Genevieve said as she gathered her half of the envelopes. "There's no reason we have to do this together."

Then she walked away with a swish of her ribboned ponytail, leaving Mihi in silence.

Over the past couple months, Mihi had been happy at home, in her own world. She felt grateful for her family in a way she never had before. And she loved Reese and Savannah. Though the magical people and creatures she'd met called her world the Grey World, to Mihi, it looked brighter than it ever had.

But sometimes—and she couldn't admit this to Reese or Savannah—Mihi missed the Rainbow Realm. She missed the magic and adventure, the feeling that she could do anything.

And right now, wounded by Genevieve's words, Mihi missed that magical world more than ever. She could almost hear the portal calling to her, just down the hall. She could *feel* the magic, as startling as an indoor breeze, reaching out to kiss her cheek.

She looked down the hallway, temptation spreading through her chest.

It was all so close.

Chapter 2

Of course Mihi wouldn't revisit the refrigerator. Of course not.

She dreamt about the realm most nights. She wondered about its secrets. And she carried a mysterious compass, a gift from an unknown friend, in her sweatshirt pocket.

But going back would be a betrayal of Reese and Savannah, who most certainly never dreamt of returning. And besides, Mihi knew how dangerous the world was. She might be tempted, but she also remembered all those near-death experiences.

She took a deep breath and tried to focus on her task.

"Need any help?"

Mihi looked up to see Savannah, smiling softly

and holding a stack of envelopes. She wore a knit hat with a giant puffball on it over her light brown hair.

Behind her, Reese carried her own stack and raised a teasing brow at Mihi. She, too, was dressed for the cold weather, with earmuffs and a big puffy jacket. Her red-framed glasses fogged in the library's warmth, and she wiped them with her sleeve. "I can't believe you got indoor recess *again*. It defies the laws of probability."

Mihi grinned at her friends, but her smile gave way to concern. "Why are you here? Did you get in trouble too?"

Savannah shook her head as she sat beside Mihi. "We just thought hanging out with you sounded nicer than outdoor recess. It's too cold, anyway."

Reese tugged off her jacket and slid into her own seat. "Plus, I asked Ms. Lavender if we could get extra credit for helping, and she said yes."

"Not that Reese needs extra credit," Savannah added.

"You never know when you'll need some extra credit!" Reese protested.

Mihi bubbled with joy. Her friends had given up recess! For *her*! "You two are better than baby birds and cotton candy *and* outdoor recess. Genevieve was here, which was kind of terrible, but she didn't want to . . ." Mihi cleared her throat. "She decided to sit at the front of the library."

Savannah's brows pinched. "I'm sorry you had to spend time with her. I know you two used to be friends."

"She's not my favorite person either," Reese said. "She was my partner for the science fair last year. Our project was on capillary action, which is when liquid flows upward, against gravity. It happens in cases where tubes or porous materials are narrow enough to cause surface tension, and it creates a suctioning effect."

Mihi nodded as if this made sense. She hoped her eyes weren't glazing over.

Reese cleared her throat. "Anyway, our teacher gave her a higher score than me—even though *I* did most of the work. He said she was a team leader, which wasn't even true. But she certainly took the credit."

Savannah *hmmed* in sympathy. "She got the lead in the play last year, and she told us, *I didn't even want it. I just can't turn off my star power.*"

Mihi sighed. "I've heard her say that."

Savannah tilted her head. "But . . . I didn't see her when we walked in."

"Yeah, we walked through the whole library to get here and didn't see her," Reese added, before lowering her voice. "But I got a weird feeling when we talked to Ms. Lavender. I think she knows about the portal. And I think she knows we went through it."

"Really?" The hairs on the back of Mihi's neck prickled. "I thought that, too, when we first came back, but she hasn't acted weird to me since."

Savannah frowned. "Me neither."

Reese hesitated. "Okay, I'll gather more information before I turn this hypothesis into a theory."

"But . . . it doesn't matter, right? Because you don't want to go back?" Mihi tried not to sound too hopeful.

"Oh," Reese said. "Well, yeah. I guess that's a good point."

Mihi ducked her head back to the envelopes to hide her disappointment, and the other girls got to work too.

Something nagged at Mihi, though. "You didn't see Genevieve at all?"

Savannah shrugged. "Maybe she went to the bathroom or something."

Mihi nodded, but worry rolled through her stomach. "I'll be right back," she blurted, pushing out of her chair and speed-walking down the hallway.

Surely everything was fine. Surely Mihi was just being paranoid.

She turned the corner into the librarian's lounge—and there, sitting on the floor next to the wide-open refrigerator, was Genevieve's backpack.

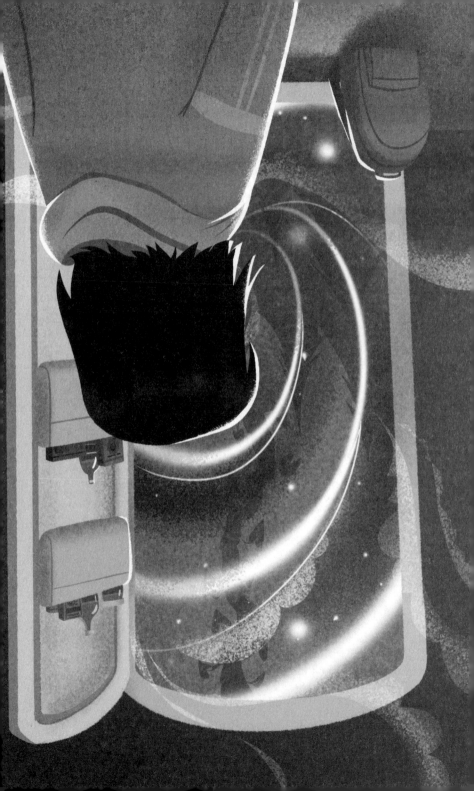

Chapter 3

The portal had already closed up. The inside of the refrigerator looked normal—unassuming—just a couple of take-out containers, a can of Coke, and a pile of rainbow candy.

But Genevieve had gone through. Mihi knew it in her bones.

"Uh, Mihi."

She heard Reese's voice behind her.

"Please tell me this doesn't mean what I think it means."

Heart rattling behind her rib cage, Mihi spun around to face Reese and Savannah. "I didn't think she'd take me seriously!"

Reese's eyes widened, and Savannah's brows pinched.

"You told Genevieve?" Savannah asked.

Mihi bit her lip. The three of them had never made a formal agreement. They'd never promised not to tell anyone. And *technically* she hadn't told. But . . . she knew she'd made a terrible mistake. "I thought I disguised it as a *story*," she said. "I was trying to cheer her up."

Savannah tugged at her hair. "Why would telling her about the Rainbow Realm cheer her up?"

"And why were you trying to cheer her up?" Reese added. "She's been so mean to you."

Mihi nodded. They made some good points. "I don't know," she said, turning back to the refrigerator. The thing was, she *didn't* know. She didn't understand her own actions. Why had she thought it would make a difference between her and Genevieve? Why had she *wanted* to make a difference? She was supposed to be done with that friendship, once and for all.

"What do we do now?" Savannah asked.

"Well, we could just hope she comes back." Reese chewed her cheek. "But that doesn't seem right."

Savannah looked at the clock. "And we know time

moves differently there. Days passed in the realm while only seconds passed here."

Reese nodded. "We need to make this decision fast."

Mihi's stomach churned. "I'll go after her."

Reese and Savannah exchanged a glance.

"But . . ." Savannah said, "it's dangerous."

"I know. But Genevieve wouldn't be in there if it weren't for me." And besides, Mihi couldn't help but feel like she owed Genevieve something. They'd been friends for so long.

Plus, part of her secretly *wanted* to return to the Rainbow Realm. She ached to feel the magic again.

"You warned Genevieve that it's dangerous, right?" Reese asked. "When you told her?"

"More or less." Mihi winced, remembering her words. *You could never survive.* She pulled the compass out of her sweatshirt. "But now I have this, which will make finding a portal back home easy."

Savannah bit her lip.

"Wish me luck," Mihi said, sliding a few extra candies into her pockets.

Reese sighed. "Oh all right. I'll come too."

Mihi hesitated. "You don't have to."

"I don't particularly like Genevieve. She's rude and a little spoiled, and she doesn't seem to care about other people's feelings," Reese said. "But . . . she's also in trouble."

Savannah chewed her lip. "And you'll need our help, Mihi. I'm coming too."

Before Mihi could respond, they both took their own pieces of candy. Mihi carefully saved her wrapper, then popped the candy into her mouth.

The familiar taste of red bean rice cakes danced on her taste buds, and the inside of the refrigerator warped like it was made of Play-Doh and the universe was stretching it apart, remolding it—until finally, it became a rainbow-colored forest.

"I will never understand that," Reese murmured.

"I've been dreaming about this place." Savannah sighed.

"You have?" Mihi asked.

The week after they returned, the three of them had discussed the Rainbow Realm constantly. But then Savannah had asked them to stop, and Mihi hadn't

pushed it. She'd figured it was because Savannah never wanted to think about it again, and though Mihi had been sad, the silence almost made things easier. If they'd talked more about it, Mihi would've confessed how much she missed the magic, and that wouldn't have been good.

"Me too," Reese said.

Mihi turned to Reese in surprise, but her friend didn't elaborate. All she said was, "Let's go."

Feeling apprehensive and—she couldn't deny it—a little excited, too, Mihi stepped into the refrigerator . . . and out through a tree in the Rainbow Forest.

For Henry,
who fights giants

❧ Chapter 4 ❧

Most times, Mihi's fond memories took on a Technicolor quality. Her idea of something often became bigger and better than its reality.

But she hadn't thought that could happen with the Rainbow Realm. The Rainbow Realm had been too perfect to hold in a memory, so Mihi assumed the color-streaked trees, the vanilla cupcake–scented breeze, and Sleeping Beauty's castle off in the distance would be even *better* if she ever returned.

But when Mihi stepped through the refrigerator, that wasn't the case.

Sure, the world was colorful. The air was warm. The breeze smelled nice.

But everything seemed a bit . . . wilted. The leaves on the trees drooped. The trunks pruned like Mihi's fingertips after a long bath. And though Mihi remembered cushiony velvet moss from last time, now the ground was hard and dry.

On top of all that, the world seemed *dimmed*, faded, as if someone had turned down the vibrancy.

"What happened?" Mihi asked as she unwrapped her scarf.

Savannah tugged off her winter hat and pointed into the distance. "Is that . . . ?"

Above the tree line, a thick green trunk twisted upward, rising straight into the clouds. Dark sap oozed from its gnarled knots like blood from a wound, and it loomed so large it cast a shadow over much of the forest.

"The beanstalk," Mihi whispered. "From Jack's story."

"That's a change," Savannah noted.

Reese raised her brows. "A lot has changed."

Mihi didn't want to think about that, so she smoothed out the candy wrapper and watched as faint lines began to appear on it. A thrill went through her at the familiar sight. "Let's figure out where we're going," she said.

Reese held her wrapper next to Mihi's, and the two pieces of foil stitched together, forming a bigger map. "Do you have any idea where Genevieve might have gone first?"

Mihi bit her lip, trying to think, but came up empty. "Sleeping Beauty's castle?"

Savannah tilted her head as she added her wrapper to the map. "Are you sure you aren't just saying that because *you* want to visit the castle?"

"I *really* want to visit the castle!" Mihi admitted. "But honestly, I'm not sure where Genevieve would have gone." The two of them used to play princesses together, back when they were still friends. But Genevieve had turned her nose up at the whole idea of princesses. Would she still be drawn to the castle? Something inside Mihi said yes, but she wasn't sure.

"Oh no," Savannah said, looking up.

Mihi followed her gaze to see a small mouse wearing thick black glasses, a grey suit, and a green tie. As he walked toward them on the road, Mihi's heart sank.

"*You*," he said when he reached them.

"Jonathan," Mihi said, glaring.

Reese took a step back. "Where are your friends?"

Last time they'd seen him, he'd been with two other mice—making the three "Great Mice," as they called themselves. They'd claimed to be the most powerful creatures in all the land, but now Mihi suspected they were just moderately powerful mice . . . who loved chaos.

The mouse turned his whiskered nose up in the air, looking, honestly, a bit like Genevieve. "I'll have you know that we are all incredibly busy individuals. We have our own affairs to attend to and are *quite* independent."

"What do you want?" Reese asked, folding her arms over her chest.

Jonathan adjusted his tie. "Why are Greys always so *hostile?*"

"Wait a minute," Mihi said, peering at his tie. On closer inspection, it wasn't a tie at all. It was a *ribbon*. A thin, green ribbon that she'd definitely seen before. "Where'd you get that?"

"I'll tell you . . ." He tilted his head, and Mihi could practically see him thinking. "If you answer a riddle."

"No way," Reese said. "The last time we fell for

one of your tricks, you stole Mihi's crown necklace, tricked us into competing for princesshood, and then tried to kill us."

Jonathan exhaled a long-suffering sigh. "That was Houdini, not me. And he shouldn't get to have *all* the fun."

Mihi narrowed her eyes and wondered about the ethics of trying to squash him.

He held up a little paw, perhaps sensing her murderous thoughts. "I swear. It's just for fun. And then I'll tell you where that blonde Grey went."

So it *was* Genevieve's ribbon.

"Fine," Mihi agreed, hoping she wouldn't regret it.

Jonathan stood a little straighter and cleared his throat. *Ahem.*

"If you stare at me, I'll stare back.
If you hit me hard, I will crack.
I flip the world, but I don't move.
I'll betray you, when you least expect me to.
Don't say I didn't warn you.
What am I?"

Mihi tried not to grin. Her little brother, Jihu, loved riddles. He told her a new one practically every day, and though she'd never particularly loved them herself (they made her brain feel fuzzy), she loved how happy they made him.

And she'd heard enough of them to know the answer.

She turned to her friends and whispered, "It's a mirror."

Savannah's eyes lit up, and she nodded. But Reese hesitated.

"That makes sense for the first three lines," she agreed. "But what about the fourth one? I'll betray you? How would a mirror do that?"

Mihi had been so excited about the first half of the riddle that she hadn't really considered that fourth line. But it didn't matter. She was sure of the answer.

"Maybe if you're having a bad hair day or something?" Savannah suggested. "And you don't want to know?"

Reese frowned. "But that's not a betrayal. That's just the mirror reflecting reality."

Mihi shook her head. "I agree with Savannah,"

she said. "Sometimes riddles don't always make exact sense. Trust me, I hear *a lot* of them."

Reese swallowed, but then nodded, and Mihi turned to Jonathan and announced, "A mirror."

For a second, Jonathan didn't answer. Then he smiled, and his razor-sharp teeth flashed. "Indeed it is."

Mihi grinned, triumphant.

"And as for the blonde," he continued, "she went to Sleeping Beauty's castle."

Reese took a deep breath. "You were right, Mihi. And I guess we do get to see the princess."

Mihi grinned with anticipation and relief, and the girls left Jonathan behind, making their way toward the castle.

It was only after they'd left that worry tickled the back of her mind. She wondered if, maybe, they should have asked Jonathan about that fourth line after all.

And though she tried to push it from her thoughts, Jonathan's voice seemed to echo behind them.

Don't say I didn't warn you.

Chapter 5

Mihi's spirits lifted as soon as she saw the castle. Like everything else in the Rainbow Realm, the grounds around the castle had changed, but here they'd changed for the better.

Before, the grounds had been perfectly maintained, so much so that nobody seemed to walk on them. Now they were full of life. Though the fields had browned like everywhere else in the forest, they were filled with *people*.

Little kids ran and played on the fields. Teenagers painted and picnicked. An older woman played the flute; a young man strummed a guitar. All around, people smiled, laughed, and traded stories.

"Everyone looks so happy," Mihi said.

Her eyes caught on a girl across the field, just slightly

older than Mihi, with her blonde hair cut short, just above her shoulders. She wore a plain blue dress instead of a ball gown—and Mihi almost didn't recognize her.

But it was her, Sleeping Beauty, lounging on a picnic blanket with a few other girls. One of them was familiar: Della, a cook who used to work in the castle.

Savannah called out. "Sleeping Beauty!"

The princess turned, and after a moment of shock, she jumped to her feet. "Savannah! Reese! Mihi!" She ran toward them, bouncing as if she were physically lighter now without that unwanted destiny weighing her down. "I thought I'd never see you again."

Mihi hugged her. "So did we."

"How much time has passed?" Savannah asked.

"A little over a year."

Mihi tried to wrap her head around that. It was strange how time warped here.

Reese gestured to the field. "A lot has changed in a year."

Sleeping Beauty nodded. "Thanks to you three, I've

tried to make my own happily ever after, and I'm try-ing to let my people do the same."

"And you haven't married a prince?" Mihi asked. She knew they were here to find Genevieve, but it still felt important to ask. She wanted to make sure the princess really was living the life she wanted.

"No way. Oh, and I'm not going by Sleeping Beauty anymore since, you know, I didn't actually sleep for very long. I've decided to go by Pat. Bertha suggested it. She said she had an old friend named Pat."

Reese raised her brows, and Savannah cleared her throat. "Are you sure? It's a little old-fashioned."

"I think it's perfect," Mihi said, meaning it. It just *fit* the princess.

Pat grinned, and Mihi's heart filled with bubbles.

"So, Bertha's still around?" Reese asked, some caution creeping into her tone. Bertha hadn't exactly been warm and friendly last time they were there.

"She's not *so* bad," Pat insisted.

Mihi wasn't sure about that.

"Really, she's been so helpful to me. I wouldn't be able to support my kingdom alone. Honestly, I'm not sure how much I can do, not with everything else that's going on."

Mihi tasted dread, bitter and burning. "What *is* going on?"

Biting her lip, Pat glanced back at her people, then pulled the girls farther away, lowering her voice. "Well, the people in the forest villages have never had much food, and I thought I could fix that. We have more than we need, so I started to give some away. But then the giant—did you see the beanstalk?"

"It's hard to miss," Reese said.

"Well, he began stealing the rain, and with the drought he's caused, our crops are dying. There's not enough food to go around."

"He started stealing the *rain*?" Reese repeated. "How is that even possible?"

"Magic," Mihi answered.

Pat nodded. "He's figured out a way to use dust to do it."

Mihi remembered the magic dust they'd used last time—ground up bits of magic, for people and creatures who couldn't use magic on their own.

Savannah's brows pinched. "But these people don't look hungry or unhappy. They're playing. They're laughing."

"For now." Pat bit her lip. "The castle has always had so much, so we have enough in reserve to care for our own. And we've been able to use some dust to stretch the food further.

"But we don't have enough for everyone. The Treehouse Village has gotten hit the hardest, and they're becoming angrier with me and my people. And my people . . . I'm worried they're getting meaner. When they see the villagers begging for food, they turn away. They respond with coldness rather than compassion." Her voice cracked, and her gaze lingered on the forest before returning to the girls. "I don't know what to do."

Mihi and her friends exchanged a glance. They'd passed the Treehouse Village last time they were here, a community of cozy houses carved into trees. Mihi remembered the sense of familiarity she'd felt. She knew what it was like to have less than her neighbors.

"And all the while, the giant sits in the clouds, blaming everyone below for not taking care of their crops."

Mihi chewed her cheek. They had to *do* something. But what could they do about a weather-stealing giant?

She racked her heart for any kind of answer. Her mind started racing. Ideas whirred . . .

But Savannah interrupted her train of thought. "I wish we could help."

"Me too," Reese said.

Right. No. They *couldn't* help. With some difficulty, Mihi reined her ideas back in. Last time, she'd gotten them into trouble by pushing ahead without Reese and Savannah. She couldn't do that again. "The giant sounds terrible, and I'm so sorry," she said. "But we're actually here to find someone."

Savannah explained, "She's our age, about Reese's height, blonde with blue eyes. Um, she kinda looks similar to you."

"One of the mice said she went to find you," Reese added.

The princess thought for a moment, then hesitated. She held her breath as though she were afraid to speak, looking a bit like Mihi felt right before she told her parents she'd gotten in trouble again.

Mihi felt prickly with dread. "Did you see her?"

"It might have been someone else, but she fits the description," Pat said slowly. "I saw her talking to someone about a week ago, on the border of my kingdom and the Treehouse Village."

"Oh dear," Mihi murmured. She was pretty sure she knew exactly who Pat was talking about. "Was she talking to a teenager with a long braid and a slightly terrifying smile?"

The princess nodded. "That's about right. But I haven't seen her since."

Reese turned to Mihi. "You know who that is?"

"I think so. She's the girl I met when I went to the Healing Orchard. She told me Goldilocks was a Grey." The girl, Maven, had made the hairs on Mihi's neck prickle. "I'm pretty sure she's Snow White's evil queen." And she was dangerous.

Chapter 6

The girls made their way toward the Treehouse Village quickly. They had no time to lose.

"So, about this evil queen . . ." Reese said as they crunched over dried, fading moss. Mihi had found the old strips of her dress, which she'd tied to the trees like a bread-crumb trail last time she was here, and they followed those, knowing they would lead them straight to the Treehouse Village—and Maven.

"Well, I'm not *positive* it's her," Mihi said. "But she had a magic mirror. She lived in an apple tree. And she talked about needing to take what she wanted."

Savannah shuddered. "She sounds terrifying."

"Yeah," Mihi agreed. "But also kind of . . . cool."

Reese raised a brow at Mihi.

"Not the potentially evil part obviously," Mihi

rushed to add. "Mostly, she was creepy. But she seemed so confident, and powerful, and . . . fearless."

"Fearless." Savannah said to herself, as if the word were a magic spell.

Reese shook her head. "Genevieve's all those things, too, and it's not always a good thing, not without kindness. If Genevieve joins forces with the evil queen . . . I don't even want to think about what could happen."

Savannah frowned. "If we lived in a fairy-tale world, Genevieve would definitely be a villain."

Mihi stepped over shriveled leaves as she considered that. Was Genevieve really a *villain*? Some days—okay, fine, a lot of days—Mihi felt that way. But her former friend had moments of kindness too. Did that make her meanness okay?

"Our world is different, though." It was the only thing she could think to say.

They picked up the pace and fell into silence as they walked, until Reese said, "I've been thinking about this world, and there's something I still haven't figured out. How have these stories been preserved for so long? And what happens when they change?"

"Zombies happen," Mihi responded, shuddering at the memory of Pat's sleepwalking, zombie-fied ladies-in-waiting.

"And it's dangerous, like Blackberry told us," Savannah said.

Mihi's heart pinched with fondness as she remembered the little bear, who'd wanted to be kinder and more generous than his parents.

Reese nodded. "Right, but are there long-term effects? The zombies were scary, but now the princess seems so happy, and everyone around her seems better off. It almost seems like the stories are *meant* to change."

"Maybe they are. I think these stories changed *me*, at least," Mihi said. A little *zing* of excitement traveled from her head to her toes, and she mustered the courage to ask, "Have you two thought about this world . . . a lot?"

Reese hesitated before nodding.

So did Savannah. "This is a special place—and a place to, I don't know . . ." She blushed. "Be special."

A lump rose in Mihi's throat. This whole time, she'd thought her feelings were wrong or strange. She'd thought she was alone. But her friends had been feeling the same way this whole time. "I feel that way too."

"I thought we could leave this place behind," Reese said. "But it's not easy to forget about magic. It's like trying to figure out the world's biggest puzzle. Which is scary, and exciting."

"If this place meant something to all of us," Mihi said, swallowing that lump, "then shouldn't we try to help the people and their world? Shouldn't we try to stop the giant?"

"But the giant is so much bigger than us," Savannah squeaked. "We're just kids."

Reese took a deep breath. "And *how* could we do that? He's controlling the rain. I didn't even know that was possible until about ten minutes ago."

Mihi bit her lip, trying to think of an adequate response. But before she could, they arrived. The Tree-house Village.

Last time, the village had been easy to miss. If none

of them had looked up to see the homes carved into trees, they would have walked right past it.

But they couldn't miss it now, because right in the center of the clearing was a thick green beanstalk, reaching up past the homes, past the trees, all the way into the sky. It was the only healthy, thriving plant for miles. Invisible waves of magic rippled around it.

Everything else, though, was dying. And the people, too—Mihi saw some families sitting on the branches of their trees, their clothes torn and dirty. There wasn't shouting and laughter here the way there was near the castle.

"We have to do something," Mihi said.

Savannah bit her lip. Reese winced. And Mihi ached to run to the families and ask them how she could help. But instead, she told herself: *focus.*

"Maven's apple tree is this way," she told her friends. "The treehouse with the red door."

They started toward the door—and then heard a soft thud behind them, followed by: "I heard my name."

Mihi recognized the voice instantly, the twinkling kind of voice that *seemed* nice, but was always just on

the verge of mocking you. A voice that said, *I know something you don't know.*

Shivering, Mihi turned and found that Maven had jumped down from a branch above them. She brushed dirt from her skirt, though it didn't help much. It was more tattered than the plain brown dress she'd worn last time, and she had streaks of dirt smudged across her cheeks, which were sunken from a lack of food.

"Either quit staring," Maven said with a sharp smile, "or tell me I look beautiful. We have limited water for baths, so we have to make do with the dirt."

"You look . . . beautiful," Mihi said, managing to sound less scared than she felt. Despite her current appearance, it wasn't untrue. Maven had the same inner sparkle that Genevieve did. It made Mihi dizzy.

Maven tilted her head. "I know you. You took an apple from the Healing Orchard a year ago. Lovely apples there."

"The apple was for me," Savannah croaked. She did *not* manage to sound less afraid.

Maven turned to Reese and Savannah, tossing them a hungry smile. "But I don't know *you*. I'm Maven."

Reese cleared her throat. "Hi, Maven. We're looking for someone, and we thought you might be able to help."

"You were talking to a girl, over by the castle," Mihi said. "Blonde hair, our age. Uh, not from around here."

Maven waved a hand. "Spare me the boring details. I already know you're looking for Genevieve, the Grey you used to be friends with, whom you still miss, even though you wish you didn't."

Reese turned to Mihi. "You miss her?"

"That's the part you choose to focus on?" Mihi asked. That wasn't like Reese—she usually pinpointed the details that would help them and let the rest fade away.

Reese half shrugged, looking a little embarrassed.

Maven raised a brow. "It *is* the interesting part, isn't it?"

"It's not." Mihi didn't meet Reese's eyes. She couldn't explain it. She *knew* Genevieve treated her poorly, but she sometimes missed their friendship anyway. It was almost comforting to know her place.

Even if that place felt cramped and uncomfortable. Turning back to the possibly-evil, possibly-future-queen, she asked, "Genevieve told you that?"

"Of course not." Maven laughed. "But my mirrors never lie."

"What—"

"I *told* her not to go up there," Maven went on. "But she insisted."

"Go up where?" But as the question left her lips, Mihi realized the answer. Her heart sank.

Genevieve had gone up the beanstalk.

Chapter 7

Maven watched as the severity of the situation dawned on Mihi and laughed.

"You've noticed this eyesore, I presume," Maven said, gesturing grandly to the beanstalk behind her.

The girls nodded.

"I've known Jack since he was a baby, and he's always been a bit dim. But I admit those beans were an impressive find. The beanstalk could be huge for our village if we use it to our advantage. It goes straight up to the giant's manor—and if we took some of his treasure, maybe we could afford to buy food again."

"Oh no," Savannah whispered, wringing her hands together.

Mihi *should* have felt wary of that flash in Maven's eyes, but then the girl's brows pinched. Genuine concern flashed across her face. "The giant has taken from us for too long, and now he's stolen the rain. If nothing changes, people will die."

"That's terrible," Reese said.

"How could he be so cruel?" Savannah murmured.

Maven's jaw hardened. "It's like he's forgotten that everyone down here exists. If he doesn't have to see us, he doesn't have to consider how much his actions hurt us."

Reese and Mihi exchanged a glance. Something about Maven's words rang in her heart.

Then Maven sighed. "Of course, I was formulating a plan to *make* him consider, and then your Genevieve showed up."

"Why did Genevieve climb up there?" Savannah asked.

Mihi *hoped* it was because Genevieve wanted to help, but that didn't really seem like Genevieve's style.

"She was asking all these questions about the beanstalk," Maven said. "And we got to talking about the giant's gold. I suppose she wanted some for herself."

"Genevieve wanted gold?" Savannah asked. "But she's . . ."

"Already rich," Reese finished.

Maven's eyes flashed. "Everyone's tempted by *more*, the rich more than anyone. I told her she'd never survive, but she didn't believe me."

Mihi bit her lip as she remembered their conversation in the library.

You could never survive this.

Were Maven's words a reminder of Mihi's? Had the way Mihi taunted Genevieve pushed her to prove Mihi wrong—the same way Genevieve's words had haunted Mihi?

You're not the princess type.

"She's been up there for a week," Maven added.

Mihi, Reese, and Savannah turned to one another with horror in their eyes.

"I'm going up there," Mihi said, pulling her friends aside. "But you two don't have to. You should go home, where it's safe."

Two months ago, she'd climbed an apple tree to prove Genevieve wrong. Now she was about to climb a beanstalk to save her.

Reese sighed. "Trying to help Genevieve feels like digging a deeper and deeper hole, because now I have to go up too. I'd feel too guilty if I didn't try. Which I hate, because I don't think she'd feel the same way for me."

"You two are good people," Savannah said softly. She closed her eyes and took a breath, as if internally debating. Finally, she opened them and said, "Okay, me too." Her voice shook.

"You don't have to," Mihi assured her.

Savannah shook her head, "No, it's fine. I'm not scared. I'm brave now, remember?"

Mihi craned her neck, trying to see the top of the beanstalk, but the clouds blocked her view. "Do you think we can stop the giant while we're up there?"

Reese pushed her glasses up her nose. "We can try."

Mihi looked up—and up. Her stomach flipped. That was *high*, and the dangerous climb would only lead to more danger. Why had Genevieve done this?

Mihi's taste buds prickled with bitterness. The Genevieves of the world always expected someone to save them. Because of course, someone always did.

Well then, fine. After this, she would never owe her former friend anything again.

She grabbed hold of the beanstalk trunk and readied herself to climb, but Maven cleared her throat.

"I wouldn't advise going *just* yet," she said. "Of course, you don't need to take my advice. I'm just an all-knowing witch."

Mihi turned back to Maven. "But Genevieve's already been gone a week."

"Exactly. She's either dead, or they've locked her up." She said this like someone might say, *She either has allergies or a slight cold.* "A couple hours won't make a difference."

Savannah tugged at her hair. Reese narrowed her eyes.

Mihi inhaled, exhaled, inhaled, exhaled, trying to keep from bolting right up the beanstalk. "Why should we wait?"

"Because the giant is throwing a huge party tonight and inviting the most fearsome creatures in all the land."

"*Excuse me?*" Reese said.

Savannah looked like she might faint. In their experience, magical balls and parties usually resulted in near death.

"Which means lots of people will be coming and going," Maven said. "The giant will be distracted."

"But we'll stand out," Mihi said. "We're obviously not fearsome."

Maven grinned. "And that, my dear Grey, is why you'll need a disguise."

Savannah bit her lip. "Do you have a disguise good enough to trick monsters?"

"*I* don't. But I know someone who does. You'll need to train with some of the best villains around."

"Villains," Mihi repeated. "You want us to waltz up to bad guys, who will train us to meet even *more* bad guys?" She did not add that they were, at this very moment, possibly speaking to a bad guy. Mihi missed the safety of Pat's castle.

Maven grinned. "Oh, please. These guys wouldn't hurt a fly." Then she paused. "Well, I suppose that's not entirely true."

Savannah squeaked.

"If you want any chance of rescuing your friend,

listen to me. Go to the Station. Find the masters of disguise. Tell them Maven sent you." She pulled three compact mirrors from her dress pocket. "Take these. They're friendship mirrors, so they're linked. They'll let you communicate if any of you are in trouble."

Hesitating slightly, the girls took the mirrors.

"Why are you helping us?" Reese asked. "It doesn't seem like you're doing this out of the goodness of your heart."

"It doesn't?" Maven asked, innocently enough to be suspicious. "Well, I suppose you don't have to trust me. But you don't have much of a choice."

Mihi turned to her friends. "I think we should listen to her," she whispered. "She's terrifying, but I don't think she's lying . . . exactly."

Savannah inhaled. "Okay. I'm with you."

Reese nodded. "According to the map, we've got a long journey ahead."

"Good luck!" Maven said, too brightly.

And then Mihi, Reese, and Savannah set out to meet dangerous villains so they could save Mihi's archnemesis—and also, possibly, the entire realm.

Chapter 8

Reese was right. The journey was long. They'd been walking for hours, and Mihi, who was not the biggest fan of hiking, hurt all over. But despite the pain, and despite the danger in front of them, Mihi still couldn't help but love this world.

It reminded her that anything was possible.

"What do you think the Station is?" she asked. "It must relate to a specific fairy tale, right?"

Reese peered at the map as they walked. "Maven said we'd be training with villains, so maybe it's a place where fairy-tale creatures go to train."

Savannah scrunched her nose. "I don't like training in this world. It didn't go so well last time."

"That wasn't *official* training, though," Mihi reassured her. "The mice told us it was princess training, but that was a trick."

"True." Savannah's shoulders relaxed. "Do you think it'll be like a school?"

Reese looked up from the map, eyes glittering behind her glasses. "Maybe there will be classes that explain the details of this world!"

Mihi grinned. Seeing her friends' excitement made her giddy.

And when they finally reached their destination, none of them could deny their wonder.

The trees cleared, and in front of them stood what looked like a stadium-sized greenhouse. It pulsed with light, almost like a beating heart.

"That doesn't look like a school," Savannah murmured.

Reese checked the map. "This is the right place, though."

"Do you think it's a sports game?" Savannah asked.

"Or a gladiator arena?" Mihi suggested as they reached the massive front doors. They'd learned about ancient Rome in school. "Like a fight to the death?"

Savannah recoiled, but Mihi pushed the doors open and found a large space filled with people. They formed a line at a booth that read TICKETS, and above them was a sign with a header that read ARRIVING SOON. Beneath that was a list of hundreds of countries.

"Of *course!*" Reese exclaimed, as if she'd missed an obvious answer on a math test. "It's a *train* station."

"A magical train station," Mihi marveled.

Sometimes, on birthday trips or special occasions, Mihi's family took the green line into Boston. That train was rickety, with its green plastic seats, and the nearest train station was made of concrete and metal, often bone-bitingly cold.

This wasn't anything like that.

For one thing, this train station was bustling. People, animals, and creatures Mihi had never seen before moved past them. Mihi saw people of all different races and species, and caught bits of different languages. Some wore royal silks and gowns. Others dressed as plainly as Maven.

"This is different," Mihi said, drinking it all in.

Reese lowered the map, looking around in awe. "This is better."

"But what fairy tale is it?" Mihi didn't know if she agreed with Reese. She loved the Rainbow Realm because it was new and familiar at the same time. The magic was strange and exciting, but comforting, too, because she recognized it.

This train station wasn't familiar at all.

But Mihi couldn't deny that it woke something in her. She felt restless, as if she was supposed to do something but couldn't remember what.

"I don't think this is a fairy tale," Savannah murmured. Unlike Reese, she looked more nervous than excited.

"It's not *a* fairy tale," Reese said. "It's all of them. From everywhere."

The circular building was lined with tunnels. Only one of them was labeled: THE BAZAAR. The others seemed to disappear into black holes.

"I'm guessing we should go to the bazaar," Mihi said. "At least, I'd rather choose that than pitch darkness."

Before Reese or Savannah could respond, a female voice spoke over a loudspeaker, quickly and loudly, blurring through so many languages that Mihi's head spun. Mihi managed to pick out some Korean, and the sound of Korean was so unexpected that it stopped her in her tracks. It was jarring—though not unwelcome—to hear the language *here*, in her magical fairy-tale world of all places, and as soon as the woman switched languages, Mihi missed the familiar sound of home.

"*Now arriving,*" the loudspeaker announced, finally, in English, "*from Vietnam, the Wishing Realm.*"

A whistle echoed from somewhere far in the distance, growing louder and louder until steam billowed from one of the dark tunnels, filling the station with the mingling scents of campfires, incense, and mist on a rainy morning—and a train burst through.

Or, not a train, exactly. At least not any train Mihi was used to.

Through the smoke, a train-sized dragon emerged, made of mechanical gears and iron. It sped across the floor, charging right toward them.

Chapter 9

The girls screamed as the train raced toward them, and Mihi grabbed her friends by the arms and yanked them back—just as the dragon barreled past. They toppled to the floor, so close that the rush of wind pulled at Mihi's hair, tugged at her clothes, so close that she could reach out and touch the steaming metal.

It skidded to a halt in front of them, and slowly, the doors on its side hissed open. The sounds of people talking, food frying, and music playing spilled out, along with people and creatures. Some were dressed in modern clothes, others in clothes that reminded Mihi a little of Korean hanboks.

Mihi stepped aside so a golden turtle could pass and almost tripped over a girl the size of her finger.

"Sorry!" Mihi yelped.

But the girl just waved a hand as if the threat of squish happened all the time.

A one-eyed bat, a cow-headed sheep, and a swarm of fireflies hurried past Mihi and began to board.

When the doors closed again, the dragon train snorted, steam spiraling from its nostrils. Then it took off again, whipping through the station and into another tunnel, its chugging getting quieter and quieter until it was gone.

The new arrivals bustled past, all of them walking, scuttling, flying toward the tunnel labeled THE BAZAAR.

Savannah looked at her friends. "I think Mihi's right. Let's follow the crowd."

The tunnel led to a staircase, which led down, down, down. The girls followed it for what seemed like too long, descending toward a warm, inviting flicker. When they finally reached the bottom, they saw hundreds of enchanted candles floating in the air.

All around them, market stalls and shops pressed tightly together, and people milled about, shopping and trading, chatting and laughing.

"It's an underground marketplace," Savannah said.

Mihi nodded. "With fairy-tale creatures from all over."

"This place isn't on the map," Reese whispered.

They walked through the winding hallways filled with tea shops and trinket stores, taverns and palm readers. And the *food*. Some sold spicy curries. Others heavy bowls of noodles. Others desserts made of fine sugar. They tasted and sampled, and even Reese—who had declared last time that she would never eat in the Rainbow Realm again—gave in to the scents and her growling stomach.

Luckily, the consequences of eating this time were not disastrous, merely delicious.

"I've never seen anything like this," Savannah said as she finished off a plantain cake. "It's kind of like a mall, but with so much more—"

"Fish!" A wooden puppet that looked suspiciously like Pinocchio burst from one of the shops, holding a basket of purple fish. "Caught fresh from the Home-sick River! Sure to make all your dreams come true!"

His nose grew an inch, and he frowned. "Well, the first part is true."

"No thank you," Mihi said, stepping around him.

Refocusing, Reese asked, "How are we supposed to find help? This place is a total maze."

A woman called out to Mihi as they passed. She held a pile of wood in her scaly hands, and sat in an unassuming booth, small and undecorated, much quieter than everything surrounding it.

Mihi felt almost hypnotized as she watched the woman press a small carving knife into the wood. Her footsteps slowed to a stop, but her friends didn't notice. They kept walking ahead, and she couldn't seem to move.

"Would you like to see your future?" the woman

asked, in an accent Mihi couldn't place. Beneath her was an etched wooden sign that read THE WITCH OF THE BIZARRE.

"No thanks," Mihi stammered, and all at once her legs worked again. She nearly tripped over herself as she stumbled to catch up with her friends.

But before she could tell them about the strange woman, she saw it: a little shop down the hall, with a sign declaring MASTERS OF DISGUISE. "We'll know it when we see it!" she exclaimed.

The girls wove past the crowd toward the shop, and a bell chimed as they stepped inside. Hats, wigs, and glasses lined the walls, along with vials of liquids, herbs, and candies. Mihi picked them up, examining their labels, things like *Eat Me!* and *Drink That One →!* and *No, Please Don't Drink Me!!*

Mihi set that one down and took a step back.

Across the room, Savannah ran her fingers along a coat that claimed to make people fall in love with the wearer, and Reese slid a thick leather tome off a bookshelf. When she opened it, it chirped in an eager British accent, "Ah, hello! So, you want to learn about

Running from the Authorities and Changing Your Identity!"

Reese yelped and shoved the book back onto the shelf. "Talking books. I don't know whether to be delighted or horrified."

A door at the back of the room swung open, and a wolf wearing grandmotherly pajamas, a night-cap, and reading glasses stepped out. "Horrified," he answered. "Those books will *not* shut up." He paused. "Unless you're thinking about buying one. In that case, delighted. Wonderful, wonderful books."

Mihi, Reese, and Savannah froze. The wolf wasn't so big, only slightly taller than Savannah, but he was utterly recognizable. The wolf who ate Little Red Rid-ing Hood.

None of the girls spoke.

Mihi turned to her friends with eyes that said, *A fairy-tale creature!*

Reese shook her head. Her face said, *Don't trust him.*

Savannah's expression said, simply, *We're gonna die.*

Behind him, the door swung open again, and a tiger emerged. He was bigger than the wolf and wore a suit and bowler hat. "Customers! We haven't had those in a while!" Then he cleared his throat. "I mean . . . we *always* have customers. Our store is *very* popular, and you  should *definitely* buy some items before they sell out."

He turned to the wolf. "Convincing?"

"Very."

"I'm working on my improv," the tiger said to Savannah.

Savannah took a step backward.

"Oh, wait, no, no." The tiger held up his paws. "I didn't mean to scare you. Conan says I scare people."

"I do *not* say that," the wolf insisted. "I said sometimes you come on a little strong. But in an endearing way."

A wolf and a tiger. Endearing. Right. Mihi knew how fairy tales with wolves and tigers usually ended.

"I'm Conan," said the wolf. "And this is my partner Dae Ho."

Dae Ho lifted his hat. "Pleased to meet you."

Mihi tilted her head, a memory sparking. "You're Korean?"

Dae Ho grinned, sharp teeth flashing. "As a red bean rice cake."

Mihi's heart banged against her ribs. She knew this fairy tale. Her grandfather told it to her. "I've heard about you."

The smile slipped from Dae Ho's face. "Oh."

"He's like the wolf," Mihi explained to her friends. "There's a Korean fairy tale where a tiger dresses up like a grandmother and tries to trick two little kids into letting him into their house—so he can eat them whole."

Savannah paled. "So, they both eat children?"

"Oh *god* no," Dae Ho said.

Conan rubbed his temples. "Those stories have followed us for our whole lives. But they aren't true."

Reese crossed her arms. "We've seen how this realm works. We know you can't escape your story, so we know that you dress up as grandmothers and try to eat unsuspecting children."

"Those stories were written *for* us," Dae Ho said. "Someone else decided what our roles should be. But we refuse to play the bad guys. That's not who we are."

Conan nodded. "It's hard to escape the stories other people have created. And it can be dangerous to try to change them—but not impossible."

"That's true," Savannah said. "Pat did it."

Conan nodded. "Now we're free to be who we want to be."

Reese tilted her head. "Free," she repeated.

Here, just like Pat, were creatures whose stories had been determined for them. For a moment, Mihi considered what that would feel like—and then she wondered if she already had an idea. Genevieve had told her she wasn't the princess type. She'd tried to decide that *for* Mihi. And that felt terrible.

"Who do you want to be?" she asked.

"Ourselves," Conan said.

His answer was so unexpectedly simple that emotion rose in Mihi's throat. She turned to her friends, who looked equally speechless.

Dae Ho gave his partner a soft smile, then turned to the girls, breaking the moment with a grin. "And thespians, of course."

Reese and Mihi frowned, uncomprehending.

Savannah raised her brows. "Actors?"

Conan turned to his partner. "Ah, look, that child speaks pretentious theater geek too!"

"Tell me," Dae Ho said, leaning over the counter, "are you in the arts as well?"

"Um." Savannah blushed bright red. "I've done a couple plays and musicals? But I was never the lead or anything . . ."

"She's great at singing," Mihi added, remembering the magic apple that had cursed Savannah to sing everything she said.

"Well, I mean, I like it," Savannah said, "but I wouldn't say I'm great at it. I'm not very talented."

"Talent is overrated!" Dae Ho said. "It's all about training."

Training. The word shoved Mihi's brain back on track.

"That's why we're here!" she said. "We were talking

to the evil—uh, Maven—about needing disguises, and she told us to find you."

Conan's ears twitched. "Maven, huh? Terrifying."

"Seriously," Reese agreed.

Dae Ho grinned. "Well, we are, in fact, *the* masters of disguise. Why do you require our services?"

"The giant is throwing a party tonight," Mihi said. "And we're gonna break in."

The wolf and the tiger stared at them.

After a moment, Conan asked, "You're going to infiltrate the giant's manor?"

Savannah nodded. "To rescue someone."

"Hopefully," Reese added.

"And return the rain to the realm," Mihi said.

"Possibly," Reese amended.

Dae Ho clapped his paws together. "A heist with a worthy cause!"

"It's not a *heist*," Reese clarified. "It's a reluctant rescue mission and a . . . redirection of weather."

"Call it what you like," Dae Ho said, grinning. "Either way, we've got some work to do."

Chapter 10

Dae Ho was thrilled about their heist-like rescue mission, but Conan wasn't so convinced.

"This is highly ambitious," he said. "Every villain in the realm will be there, not to mention the guards and the security the giant has. And these are creatures who have *embraced* villainy, rather than rejected it."

Mihi gulped. When he put it that way, it did sound rather ambitious. But . . . "We have to rescue Genevieve. And the people of the forest are starving."

Conan sighed. "You're right. Life without rain has been bleak in the Rainbow Realm. But we can't allow three children to enter such a dangerous situation."

"Maven said sneaking in during a big event would be easier. We'll be okay," Mihi said, and she believed it. Kinda.

Dae Ho chimed in. "She does have a point. There will be so many people coming and going . . ."

Conan hesitated. "You'll have to blend in. You'll have to think like a villain. We can help you out now, but once you're there, you'll be on your own."

"You won't help us at the party?" Mihi asked.

The wolf and tiger exchanged a glance, and Dae Ho took a breath. "I can't leave the bazaar because I'm not from here. Every fairy-tale realm has its own rules about who can enter, and this realm has strict ones."

"The Station doors are enchanted," Conan explained, bitterness creeping into his voice. "Dae Ho literally can't step out."

Mihi looked out the shop window, back at the bustling market stalls. That explained why she hadn't seen anybody like this outside of the Station.

"Even if he *could* leave, we wouldn't have been invited," Conan added. "We aren't exactly fearsome."

"And as glorious as this party sounds—a soiree in a sky castle, surrounded by all the best food, entertainment, and decorations money can buy—" Dae Ho cleared his throat, then grew serious. "We wouldn't have attended. The giant's actions don't align with our values. Plus, when people get mad at him, he's always pointing the finger at creatures like us, trying to distract people by deflecting the blame."

As he thought of the giant, a ripple of anger passed across Conan's face, and for the first time, he looked truly scary. Then he looked at the girls, and his expression softened. "Okay, what you're doing is noble. Dae Ho's right. We'll do our best to help you."

"Excellent!" the tiger said. "So, disguises!"

He plucked an orange hat dotted with jingle bells off a shelf and asked Conan, "What about this, for the short child?"

Mihi frowned.

Conan sighed. "We don't want them calling *more* attention to themselves."

As they debated costume choices, Savannah pulled Reese and Mihi aside. "The wolf's disguise in Little Red Riding Hood was pretty obvious," she whispered.

"So was the tiger's," Mihi said.

Reese grimaced. "Their disguises might not help much."

Mihi had to agree, but before she could say anything, Dae Ho and Conan interrupted, arms full of decorative masks.

"We've heard the party will be a masquerade," Conan said, "which is good news for you."

"And for us," Dae Ho said. "Because it's the best kind of party to style for. Now without further ado . . ."

With a flourish, he handed Reese a mask with a gold bird beak and a burst of blue and green feathers.

"This is . . ." Reese took it, turning it over in her hands, "actually really cool."

"Of course it is," Dae Ho said.

"And for you . . ." Conan placed a brilliant snakeskin mask into Savannah's palms.

She grinned. "It's beautiful."

"And the best for last," Dae Ho said. "I've been saving this for a special occasion."

He gave Mihi a white fox mask. Its fur was soft in her hands.

"Foxes are powerful creatures where I come from," he told Mihi, "and one of them donated her winter coat to make this. I thought you might appreciate it."

Mihi loved it instantly. Mihi's grandfather had told her tales of magical foxes, just like he'd told her the tiger's story, and her heart ballooned as she thought about sitting next to him on the couch, listening to him spin his tales.

From what she remembered, foxes were usually women who shape-shifted between fox and human forms. And though they were usually the bad guys in stories, Mihi had always felt drawn to them. They were clever, and they walked between worlds. Maybe they weren't actually bad—they were just miscast, like Conan and Dae Ho.

"It's got some special abilities," the tiger added. "When you wear it, you'll get a boost of speed and strength."

The fur seemed to wink in the light.

"Thank you," Mihi said. "This means a lot."

For a moment, Dae Ho looked like he might cry. Then he cleared his throat and said, "Of course, you can't merely rely on costume work. Acting is about truly *embodying* your subject. You have to think like a villain. Walk like a villain. Talk like a villain. Understood?"

"Kind of," Mihi said.

"I guess." Reese shrugged.

"Maybe?" Savannah asked.

"Confidence, girls!" Dae Ho insisted. "Confidence is power. Pretend you have neither worry nor fear!"

Was that what being a villain felt like? The last time Mihi was here, she'd thought being a princess meant living an easy, simple life—but when she met Pat, she learned that wasn't exactly true.

Was *this* the path to an easy life? Being the bad guy? Stealing from others without a care in the world?

As Dae Ho placed the costumery into a bag, Conan plucked a small glass vial from the shelf and handed it to Mihi. "Take this too. To eat."

Reese leaned over to examine the vial, which contained what looked like a fig leaf. "The label says, *Definitely do not, under any circumstances, ever eat me*," she said.

"Oh, yes, that. That's just to discourage people from wandering in and eating expensive magic," Dae Ho reassured her.

Definitely do not, under any circumstances, ever eat me

Reese tilted her head, not at all reassured.

"The costumes will help, but this is key," Conan said. "It will let you transform into anyone—or anything—for six hours."

"Oh." Reese perked up. "So, now we *actually* have a chance of sneaking in."

Dae Ho gestured to the costumes, looking a bit offended, but Conan nodded. "This is finicky magic, though," he said, "made from figs fermented in magic dust. It requires a deep secret to activate. As soon as you uncork it, you must whisper a secret into the vial, something you've never told anyone, something you're afraid to admit, even to yourself. After you've done that, think of the most fearsome creature you can imagine, and when you eat the leaf, it will transform you."

"Do you have two more of those?" Savannah asked.

Dae Ho shook his head. "These are hard to get. We had to trade six gorgeous hats for that."

"But if you split it into thirds, it should work the same," Conan said. "It'll just last each of you two hours."

"And you'll all have exactly the same disguise," Dae Ho added. "But the masks will make that less obvious."

"I think this will work," Savannah said, and then blinked, as if her optimism surprised her.

Mihi grinned. "Let's go climb that beanstalk."

"Excellent!" Dae Ho handed Mihi the bag of costumes, and Conan walked over to the cash register, tapping keys before looking back up.

"That will be two hundred gold pieces," he said.

The bag suddenly felt very heavy.

Mihi had only been in this position once before, but she remembered it vividly. She'd been shopping for back-to-school clothes with her mom, and she'd found a pair of sparkling sneakers on the sale rack. Mihi had been thrilled. What a find! Shoes were usually boring, but these were *princess* shoes.

Only, they'd been placed on the sale rack by mistake.

She still remembered her mom's face when the cashier rang them up. Her mom had looked *guilty*, as if *she* were responsible for Mihi's crashing disappointment. The worst part was Mihi had almost *wanted* it to be her mom's fault—because at least then she'd have someone to blame. Instead, she thought, *This is the way things are, and this is the way they'll always be.* She'd tried to hide her own emotions, because she didn't want to make her mom feel even worse as they put the shoes back on the rack.

Three days later, Genevieve had shown up at school with those same exact sneakers. Mihi never said anything.

"We don't actually have . . . money," she told Conan.

Conan's smile began to wilt, like a flower without rain.

"Maybe we can trade something?" Reese asked. "When we met the mice, Mihi traded her necklace—"

"You traded with the mice?" Dae Ho interrupted, his expression growing serious.

"Yes?" Mihi answered, though based on how they were gaping at her, she had the feeling they wouldn't like that answer.

Reese frowned. "Should we be worried?"

"No, no. No no no." For an actor, Dae Ho was a terrible liar.

Mihi swallowed. "I'd really like to get it back one day. The necklace was a gift from my mom. It meant a lot to me."

Conan's eyes softened with sympathy. "I hope you do get it back one day. It's never a good idea to give those mice your belongings. Especially not belongings with sentimental value."

Mihi's stomach twisted. She didn't like how concerned they looked. It made her nervous. But right now, they needed to focus on the giant.

"Well, we don't have any money; we don't have any way to pay for the disguises." Her voice cracked. "Is there anything we can do?"

A silent communication passed between Conan and Dae Ho. Dae Ho's eyes were filled with sadness and sympathy and, also, hope. Conan nodded.

Finally, the wolf turned to the girls and said, "If you're trying to return the rain, that's more than enough. Consider this our contribution to the cause."

Mihi felt so grateful she could cry. "Thank you," she said.

Dae Ho grinned, positively giddy. "Our first sale! Well, donation, I suppose—but still! Time to restock the shelves!" He disappeared into the back storeroom.

Conan glanced at the closed door, then dropped his voice to a whisper. "Dae Ho wouldn't approve of me telling you this, because he thinks she's too dangerous, but before you break into the giant's manor, you should visit one more place first."

Mihi hesitated. "We don't have much time."

"You don't have to go far," he said. "But if you're trying to rescue someone, you'll need to know the giant's manor inside and out. And there's only one person who can help you with that."

Goose bumps skittered over Mihi's arms as he spoke.

He leaned closer. "The witch of the bizarre."

Chapter 11

Mihi led Reese and Savannah back to the witch, maneuvering through market stalls until she found the woman with light brown skin, braided crown of green hair, and blue scales from her fingertips to her elbows, like a pair of glamorous gloves.

When they approached her booth, the rest of the market seemed to fade away, as if the light and volume were on a dimmer switch. It made Mihi's head feel a little fuzzy.

"Excuse me," she said. Even her own voice sounded softer.

The woman didn't look up from the wood and knife in her hands. "What brings you to the witch at the bottom of the world?" She spoke in a deep, rumbling rhythm, almost like she was purring her words.

"The wolf sent us here," Mihi said. "Conan."

The distance between the girls and the witch seemed to elongate. Neither of them moved, but the world stretched, and suddenly, the witch was about twenty feet away. Mihi looked at her friends. Savannah's eyes were wide, and Reese rubbed her temples.

"I'm not even going to try to make sense of this," she mumbled.

Mihi figured that was the best course of action, and walked forward, closing the distance again. Now the rest of the bazaar seemed even farther away. When she looked behind her, she didn't see it at all. Her palms began to sweat.

The woman spoke as if nothing strange had happened. "Friends of Conan's are friends of mine, though he doesn't send visitors my way very often." She remained focused on her work, carving wood into art. "Today, I'm calling myself Nev, but I go by many names. You can call me whatever you'd like."

"Hi, Nev," Reese said, taking a breath to steady herself. "We're trying to . . . find our way around the giant's manor at his party tonight. We're hoping you have a map of the building or something."

The distance stretched between them again, and the girls closed the gap. Now Mihi could hardly remember they'd been in the bazaar at all. It was almost as if they were moving backward in time, toward a much older kind of magic.

"Ah, yes, the giant's grand, villainous party. I won't be in attendance, though some believe I'm the scariest villain of all." Her lips lifted into a rueful smile. "It depends who you ask."

Mihi knew that should have frightened her, but she couldn't find it in herself to be scared. Nev didn't seem scary. She just seemed sad.

"Why aren't you going to the party?" Savannah asked.

"There are many kinds of villains." Wood shavings fell to the ground as she spoke. "Some hide in plain sight, disguised as a friendly face. Some live in castles on the clouds, looming over the people they steal from. And others were never really villains at all. They were just powerful enough to know themselves, to be themselves, and someone decided that was dangerous."

Reese made a little noise in the back of her throat, and Mihi turned to her friend. For a moment, the expression on Reese's face matched Nev's—sad and hurt and a little bit angry. Then Reese met Mihi's eyes, and she swallowed, and her strange expression disappeared. Mihi didn't fully understand it, but she gave Reese a small smile to say, *I'm here.*

Reese gave a small smile back.

"I never wanted to be a villain, and I don't make it a point to socialize with those who relish the label," Nev said, tilting her head. "So, tell me, why would you want to attend that party?"

Reese hesitated. "We're trying to help someone. Multiple someones, actually."

"We're trying to return the rain," Mihi said.

Nev finally looked up, and the world around them seemed to become more *real.* The earth felt solid beneath Mihi's feet again. "I pride myself in knowing things before they happen," Nev said, "but I didn't see that coming. I like you three." She moved her hands even faster, whittling away at the wood. "I believe I can help with what you're looking for. I specialize in knowing powerful things about powerful people."

She set down her knife and handed them the piece of wood. In just those few minutes, she'd carved it into a tiny castle, and when Mihi took it, she realized the roof lifted right off.

It was as if she were peering into a little dollhouse, with intricate rooms and hallways.

"An exact replica of the giant's manor," the witch explained.

"Wow." Mihi marveled at all the details. "Have you been there before?"

"No. But this is accurate."

"How do you know?" Reese asked as she inspected the miniature manor.

"The giant," the witch said, "is so confident in the way he sees the world that he doesn't realize how many blind spots he has. Many people work for him, guarding and cleaning his manor. He looks down on them, and sometimes he doesn't notice them at all. Which means they have gathered a lot of information about him—and they talk. When they come through this market, I make it a point to listen."

Savannah frowned. "My dad is a doorman at a fancy building, and I've seen people walk past him like he's not even there."

Nev nodded. "Those who forget how to see others make a hard-hearted mistake."

A lump rose in Mihi's throat, but she swallowed it away.

"The wood will help you find your way, and it should provide you with a bit of luck too," Nev said. "Rowan wood."

Savannah's eyes widened. "I've heard of that. One of my great-aunts said it protects against witchcraft."

The corners of Nev's lips lifted. "Is that what Greys are saying now?"

Mihi glanced at her friends, who raised their brows in response. Not many people could tell they were Greys just by looking. The only other person who had was Maven.

But maybe they shouldn't have been surprised the witch could tell. She seemed to know everything about everyone.

"Rowan wood *is* witchcraft," Nev said. "Your people are so fearful of magic that they've forgotten witchcraft can be protection and healing too."

The wood warmed in Mihi's palm, and the miniature castle grew—another room here, another spire there. "What's happening?" she asked. "Why is it changing?"

"I don't question the wood. I trust it," Nev said. "Now two more gifts before you go."

The witch plucked a wooden watch from her carving table and handed it to Reese. "I haven't seen many young people wearing a timepiece, so this is for you. As I'm sure you've learned, the thread of time between our worlds is a fraying one. It's hard to control how much time will have passed when you enter. This will help."

Reese's eyes widened. "How does it work?"

The witch didn't answer, but her eyes sparkled with amusement.

Reese sighed. "Magic?"

"But of course," she responded. "When you are leaving this world, press the button on its side, and the worlds will move at the same pace. The same amount of time that passes in the Grey world will pass here."

Reese slipped off her watch and placed it in her pocket before clasping the new one on her wrist. The wooden gears began to glow and turn, and Reese stared at it like it was the most fascinating puzzle she'd ever encountered.

Nev turned to Savannah. "And for you, my dear, I will offer advice."

Savannah forced a smile, but Mihi could sense her disappointment. Mihi had gotten an enchanted dollhouse. Reese had gotten a magical watch. Advice sounded . . . well, less magical.

Nev must have sensed it, too, because she said,

"Don't fret. Words can be the most valuable thing of all."

Savannah took a deep breath and nodded.

"Eventually, you will find yourself at a crossroads between changing your truth and accepting it. You must accept it—or face dire consequences. This will not come soon, but it will come sooner than expected. Be aware. Your journey is far from over."

Though the advice was not meant for her, Mihi shivered nonetheless.

Savannah managed a thank-you, eyes wide.

"Now you have what you need," Nev said. "I'll send you where you need to go. Close your eyes."

Mihi did as she was told, and the world tore apart.

Chapter 12

Mihi loved the magic of the Rainbow Realm. But she hated teleporting.

It made her bones hurt and her brain itch, and she felt entirely powerless as the world zipped and re-arranged around her.

Finally, they found themselves at the base of the beanstalk.

The daylight was dwindling, and Mihi rubbed her arms as the air grew colder. She wished she hadn't tossed her winter clothes aside.

"Nowhere to go but up," Reese murmured, tilting her head toward the clouds.

"Let's disguise ourselves first," Savannah said. "Mihi, will you do the honors?"

Mihi nodded, her nerves mingling with excitement

as she pulled the *Definitely do not, under any cir-cumstances, ever eat me* vial from her pocket. This was *magic*. There would be time for fear when they climbed, but for now, she wanted to savor this. She'd learned to love her real home, with the everyday magic of seeing her grandmother kiss her grandfather on the cheek, or watching her parents find a new home for an abandoned kitten, or listening to her brother talk about the latest thing he learned in math class. But still. *This* magic thrilled her.

She uncorked the vial, and the scent of Fig Newtons wafted out, followed by the now-familiar porcupine-prickle of magic tickling her nostrils.

Conan and Dae Ho said the spell needed a secret—but Mihi wasn't exactly the secret-keeping type. Secrets fizzed inside her like shaken-up soda, desperate to escape, and she usually blurted them out. What did she have left? She searched the tunnels of her heart until she found something unexpected and sharp and true.

She didn't want to say it out loud, so she cupped her hands around her mouth and the vial, whispering the words right onto the leaf without her friends overhearing.

"I'm afraid that even after meeting Reese and Savannah, even after learning that I don't have to be the princess type, I'll still never be as good as Genevieve. I'll still never know how to . . . survive and thrive. And I don't know how to make that feeling go away."

The vial buzzed in her hand. Her heart tumbled as she fumbled to hold it, catching it just before it slipped through her fingers. The porcupine prickles in her nose got stronger, and she sneezed.

Focus. *Focus.* She was supposed to think of a good disguise. Something that scared her. She thought of monsters and villains, silhouettes in the dark, and shadows under the bed. Of failing out of school and never measuring up to her younger brother, and of the feeling she got when Genevieve looked at her and just *sighed*.

She willed the leaf to transform them into a creature so terrifying that they'd fit right in. They'd survive and thrive.

"Oh my goodness," Savannah said when the leaf began to glow.

Reese leaned forward to examine it. "I think it worked."

Mihi tipped it from the vial so it fell onto her palm. It felt like velvet. "So, we split it three ways?"

Reese frowned at the thought of eating more enchanted food. "Just take a little bite."

Mihi ate a third. Then Reese. Then Savannah.

They waited.

"Is something supposed to happen?" Savannah whispered.

The words were barely out of her lips when Mihi felt it.

Not pain, exactly, but . . . a loss of control, as if every bone in Mihi's body had turned to rubber. She struggled to stand and stumbled forward, feeling like, if she let herself, she might melt into the ground. Her skin began to glow. Light radiated out of every pore, so bright she had to squint.

The rubber feeling turned to Play-Doh, and suddenly she was being stretched and squashed. She felt as if everything that made her *Mihi* was being re-molded, as if her very being was a two-year-old's art project.

Slowly, so slowly, she regained control of her limbs. And when the light faded, she stared at her hands. They were . . . still hands. No claws or paws or monstrous tentacles. But they were not *her* hands. These hands were soft and delicate, free of the ink smudges and dry patches Mihi always had. These nails were *painted*, something Mihi had always envied, though her mom told her nail polish was too time-consuming.

She lifted a strand of her hair—but it wasn't *her* hair. It was blonde and silky.

The light around her friends finally dimmed, and Mihi gasped.

She had turned them all into Genevieve.

Chapter 13

"*Genevieve?!*" Reese cried. Her voice still sounded like her own, but she, too, looked exactly like Mihi's former friend. She shoved her glasses up onto her now-blonde hair. Genevieve, of course, had perfect vision. "*Genevieve* was the scariest thing you could imagine?"

"No!" Mihi protested.

"Were you picturing her?"

"No!" How had she gotten this so terribly wrong? "Maybe? By accident? I don't know!"

"It's not Mihi's fault," Savannah said uncertainly. "The magic just didn't work."

"It did work," Reese said, gesturing to their transformation. "Unfortunately."

Savannah looked down at herself. "Genevieve is so short."

Mihi shook her head. "You're just tall."

"Let's focus on the main problem." Reese attempted to push her glasses up her nose, then sighed when she remembered she wasn't wearing them anymore. "Regardless of *fault*, we are about to climb up a beanstalk and attend a monster party. But instead of disguising ourselves as monsters, we *still* look like human children."

Mihi winced.

"And do you know what monsters do to human children?" Reese continued. "They eat them. That's kind of the whole point of fairy tales."

Savannah tugged at her hair—which was now Genevieve's hair. "Oh no, oh no, no, no."

"We'll figure this out," Mihi insisted. Though their voices still sounded like Reese and Savannah, staring at two Genevieves was incredibly disconcerting. Mihi's brain told her something was really wrong, as if she'd hit her head and was seeing double. Her heart told her to run—one Genevieve caused enough hurt. But *two*?

She squeezed her eyes shut and took a deep breath. Reese was right. This was a problem. "Okay, the plan is . . . not as great as it was five minutes ago."

She reached into her pockets, pushing past Maven's magic mirror and Nev's dollhouse until she found the compass. She pulled it out and flipped it open, and the arrow spun before landing on Maven's tree. A portal home was right there, just a few steps away. They could leave.

And a small part of Mihi, one she felt rather ashamed of, wanted to.

When she thought about Genevieve, she felt frustrated. Why should Mihi put herself in danger to help Genevieve, who had never been particularly nice to Mihi, despite their many years of friendship?

But . . . this wasn't just about Genevieve. This was about Princess Pat and the Treehouse Village and Dae Ho and Conan and Blackberry and his bear family and everybody who lived in the Rainbow Realm. And this was about the Rainbow Realm itself—a world that showed Mihi what was possible.

Because of this world, because of magic, she really, truly, believed it was possible to stop a giant.

"Wait!" she exclaimed. "We still have the masks!"

She slipped the fox mask over her face and turned to her friends. "Can you still tell I'm a kid?"

Savannah hesitated. "Um . . ."

"Definitely," Reese said, her eyes sliding to the compass in Mihi's palm. She seemed to be doing a calculation of her own. Then she shook her head. "But this might be our only option. And there's no going back now. I didn't get turned into *Genevieve Donnelly* just to turn around and go home."

Savannah chewed her lip, then slipped the snakeskin mask over her face. "At least the mask is better than nothing."

The knot in Mihi's chest loosened. Everything was easier with them by her side. Especially when the masks kept them from looking exactly like her archnemesis.

"Okay. Let's climb." Mihi grabbed hold of the stalk and hoisted herself up. She looked to the sky, at the beanstalk that disappeared into the clouds.

They had a long way to go.

So they began.

"Reese?" Mihi asked, after they'd climbed for about fifteen minutes. They were already so high that she was afraid to look down. "How would you calculate our odds of success?"

Savannah gulped. "I don't want to know the answer."

But Reese narrowed her eyes, thinking, and then she almost laughed. "With anybody else, I'd say they're terrible. But with the three of us . . . I think we might just have a chance."

Chapter 14

ihi felt, to put it gently, like her head was about to explode. Her muscles shook, and as they climbed in altitude, her ears had popped about fifty times.

They'd finally reached the clouds, and they breathed in mist that tasted like butterscotch and moss.

"Do these clouds seem strange to you?" Reese asked. "Other than the fact that they're . . . flavored."

Mihi tried and failed to remember the water cycle unit from school. "How so?"

"If the giant is preventing rain from falling, the clouds should feel dense and wet," Reese explained. "But they feel almost dry."

"Weird," Savannah whispered.

A thick sense of foreboding grew in Mihi's chest.

But they kept climbing until they reached the top of the clouds.

"There it is," Savannah said. Like the other girls, she was out of breath, and her words came out in wisps, but she pointed to the manor.

It towered above them, made of glass so sharp and smooth that it reflected the setting sun. Mihi shielded her eyes with her hand.

On each spire was a carved glass statue. At first, they appeared to be gargoyles—but upon closer inspection, Mihi realized they were *geese*, with their wings spread wide and their beaks open, as if in mid-attack.

"Those geese are the creepiest things I've ever seen," she said.

"Mihi," Savannah murmured. "Those geese statues are the least creepy thing about this situation."

"You have a point."

They weren't the only ones at the giant's manor. Around them, party guests were arriving in dragon-drawn carriages, appearing in puffs of purple smoke, materializing in shadow like the nightmares they were.

Mihi saw ghosts, goblins, and witches—so very

many masked witches, holding cauldrons and broomsticks, some in tattered robes, others in ball gowns, and one in sequined overalls. Mihi recognized some creatures from stories she'd heard, but there were many more.

She tightened her grip on the beanstalk as her heart threatened to burst from her chest.

"What do we do?" Savannah squeaked, any hint of confidence evaporating in the blinding light of the manor.

"I—I think we can walk on the clouds," Mihi said, watching as the masked villains walked around them.

"That defies the laws of physics," Reese informed them automatically.

"But these are magic clouds," Mihi said.

Reese sighed. "Yes, of course they are."

Mihi summoned all her reckless energy. How many times had she run off, climbed a rickety tree, pursued a terrible idea? This was just another in a long list. She'd survive.

She took a breath and stepped off the stalk. For a moment, her heart was in freefall. What if she was wrong? What if magical fairy-tale creatures could walk on clouds, but not regular kids?

But then her foot landed on a cloud, sticking to it like melted marshmallow, and she couldn't help but grin. "It's safe," she said. And then: "I'm walking on a *cloud*."

Reese followed. Then, with some effort, Savannah managed to pry herself from the beanstalk.

"I may never understand this place," Reese said, leaning over to dip her finger in a cloud, "but I want to try."

"Reese," Savannah whispered. "We have to blend in. Nobody else is paying attention to the clouds."

Reese straightened. "Blend in with the bloodthirsty monsters. Right."

"We don't know that they're *all* bloodthirsty," Mihi pointed out.

Reese snorted. "Oh good. Maybe only *some* of them want to eat us."

"This conversation isn't making me feel bett—" Savannah began to say, but a voice behind them cut her off.

"Excuse me," it rasped.

Mihi jumped and turned to see a troll, dressed in a blue ball gown and a glittering mask, towering over them. "I *love* your costumes."

Reese and Savannah froze. After a few hoarse attempts, Mihi found her voice. "Oh—ah—th—thank you."

"Hilarious, to dress up like the dessert."

Reese cleared her throat. "The . . . dessert?"

"The girl he found. The one he promised in a pie?" The troll tilted her head. "Isn't that what you're going for?"

"Yes, of course!" Mihi said, a little too loudly. "We're known for being . . . hilarious. That's what everyone says! Ha ha! Ha ha ha! We win costume contests, like, every year!"

Too much, Mihi chided herself. *Definitely too much.*

"*Hmm.*" The troll's smile faded. Mihi told herself, very sternly, not to faint. She could do this.

The troll leaned forward until her nose hairs were nearly touching Mihi's shoulder and inhaled deeply. "You . . . smell like real children."

Savannah made a tiny squeak that sounded suspiciously like, *We're gonna die?*

"It's perfume," Reese managed. "Very expensive." Then she linked arms with Mihi and Savannah and tugged them toward the castle. They hurried away from the troll, leaping from cloud to cloud like wispy stepping-stones to their doom. Mihi felt her whole world tilt when she looked down. In the darkness, she couldn't see the colorful fantasyland beneath her, but she knew it was far, *far* down. Her vision blurred with fear.

She tightened her grip on Reese's arm and looked ahead.

"Should we really be running toward the castle's front entrance?" Savannah asked. "There must be another way in."

"You were right about blending in," Reese said. "We haven't called too much attention to ourselves yet, so we should just follow the crowd. Besides, that troll might try to eat us if we stop."

"I don't want to be eaten," Savannah said, which Mihi felt was kind of stating the obvious.

They ran-hopped toward the castle until they

reached the double glass doors—and found themselves in the grandest party Mihi could have imagined.

Tuxedoed waiters poured fizzy drinks into goblets, and the liquid seemed to shift colors, like a rainbow in a bottle. Elaborate glass sculptures of birds (mostly geese but also ducks, swans, and, oddly, parakeets) filled every corner. A band played lively music on a transparent glass stage, and a harpist sat in a corner, playing for anyone who wandered nearby.

Whenever someone came close enough to the harp, they seemed almost enchanted, *compelled* to listen. Even at this distance, Mihi felt herself leaning toward the harp. It reminded her of the way she felt when she'd first heard the music of the Homesick River.

She took a step away.

This was a dangerous, frightful party.

But . . . it was a beautiful one. Creatures of all shapes and sizes danced, laughed, and prowled in their party masks and sparkling clothes.

And everything was big, grand, *giant*.

"Wow," Mihi breathed.

She felt out of place in every way—and it wasn't just the danger. She also had the feeling she often got around Genevieve, like she'd missed some important life lesson and didn't know the right answer.

But then she remembered. For the next two hours, she *was* Genevieve! Maybe she could borrow some of her archnemesis's confidence. Maybe, for this two-hour enchantment, she could belong somewhere fancy.

"Come here," Reese hissed, gesturing toward an enormous goose sculpture. "Do you see that?"

Mihi and Savannah ducked into a corner with Reese,

partially hidden by the giant goose. It was so big that it seemed to be growing taller, looming larger.

"See wha—" Mihi started, but then she did. The goose actually *was* growing taller— slowly, so it wasn't obvious. But it was definitely growing.

Tendrils of mist rose from the ground beneath them and seeped into the sculpture, thickening the glass. And as

Mihi looked around, she realized it wasn't just the goose. Those tendrils rose all around them, barely noticeable, just slight wisps, seeping into every corner and crevice in the manor.

"What's happening to the glass?" Savannah asked.

"It's not glass," Reese said. "It's *ice*."

An epiphany shivered down Mihi's spine, cold as the giant's manor. "The *rain*."

Reese nodded. "I think, somehow, the giant found a way to siphon the moisture from the clouds. Instead of letting it fall in the form of rain, he's using it to re-inforce his castle—and make it bigger. Which explains why that little dollhouse keeps growing."

Savannah shuddered. "So, how do we stop him?"

Mihi thought for a moment. "Maybe Genevieve's seen how it works."

"Maybe?" Reese said. "She's been here for a week, so at the very least, she's seen more than we have."

Savannah chewed her lip. "Even if she does know more, would she help us?"

Mihi hesitated. Her heart caught around the word, *No*. But she didn't know that for sure, did she? Despite

Genevieve's faults as a friend, she wasn't a terrible person. Wouldn't she help them if it meant helping so many people? "I'm not sure," Mihi admitted. "But I hope so."

Reese looked unconvinced but said, "Well, we committed to rescuing her either way, so we might as well do it. Hopefully she helps. And if not, we'll figure it out on our own."

That made enough sense to Mihi. She pulled the miniature wooden manor out of her pocket. "The troll said Genevieve would be dessert, which means she's probably in the kitchen." She searched the minuscule manor until she found a tiny room, complete with a tiny wooden stove, oven, and sinks. The wooden castle looked much less menacing than the real-life one. It gave her a small amount of comfort.

"We're close to the kitchen," Mihi said. "So, we just have to make it through this great hall and the dining room."

"That wouldn't be so bad if it weren't for the crowd of monsters in front of us," Savannah pointed out.

"We'll need a distraction." Mihi surveyed the

room until her eyes fell on the harp—which now sat abandoned. "When the harpist was playing, people seemed mesmerized. *More* than mesmerized. I think the harp might be enchanted."

She tried to recall the details of this fairy tale. She didn't know it as well as the princess stories. "There's a magical harp in 'Jack and the Beanstalk,' but I'm pretty sure that one plays itself."

"Well, this one seems to need a musician," Reese said.

"And one of us should play it," Mihi finished. "Does anyone know how?"

None of them did.

"I—I'll play it," Savannah said.

Reese and Mihi exchanged a glance.

"Really?" Mihi asked.

Hurt bristled over Savannah's face. "My grandpa used to play classical music. I think—I think some of the songs had a harp. I can figure it out."

"I mean, I definitely believe you can," Mihi added in a rush, feeling a little guilty. "You just seemed scared."

"I'm not always scared anymore," Savannah said.

"I'm—I'm different now, after the last time we came here. At least . . . I was supposed to be."

"Savannah," Reese said carefully. "You're not *supposed* to be anything. It's perfectly reasonable to feel scared right now. In fact, it would be very strange *not* to."

"I know," Savannah said. "But I want to be brave. Let me be brave." She looked down at her blonde Genevieve-curls again and straightened her shoulders. Mihi wondered if she, too, was drawing some confidence from looking like Genevieve.

"Okay," Mihi said. "So you'll cause the distraction. Meanwhile, I'll find a way to sneak into the kitchen . . ."

"And I'll be the lookout," Reese finished, grabbing Maven's mirror from her pocket. "We can use these to keep in touch."

Mihi and Savannah pulled out their own mirrors. When they opened theirs, instead of seeing themselves, they saw each other, like FaceTime, except without any sound. So, a less good version of FaceTime. But still. *Magic* FaceTime.

"We're ready," Mihi said. "Now or never."

The girls steeled themselves, ready to face the monsters.

But before they could do anything, they heard the *clink clink* of metal against crystal.

All around them, the room fell silent, and thunderous footsteps echoed off the walls.

When Mihi peeked around the goose statue, she saw the giant. He was not a horrifying ogre like the fairy tale had led her to believe. Really, he just looked like a thirty-foot-tall man with pale skin, clean-cut dark hair, and a black suit. Actually, he kind of resembled Genevieve's dad.

He towered over even the biggest party guests. In his hand, he held a Mihi-sized crystal goblet, and he tapped a knife against it to make a toast. A grin spread across his face, and when he spoke, his voice was so loud and deep that it reverberated in Mihi's chest, like a bass beat rolling out of a sports car.

"Good evening, my fearsome creatures," the giant boomed. "There is something I'd like to say."

Chapter 15

The music quieted. Creatures stopped dancing. Guests whispered among themselves, but nobody dared to speak over the giant.

Mihi, Reese, and Savannah couldn't go anywhere now. They were stuck.

"If I've invited you here, that means I admire your ambition," the giant said, swirling the rainbow fizz inside his goblet. Mihi wondered if his glass, too, was made of ice. "You've done what few others have had the courage to do. You've gained power. And though some might say you inspire fear, I simply say you *inspire*."

Something in his voice made Mihi's stomach curdle. He used the same tone that her least favorite teachers used when they assumed Mihi wouldn't understand the assignment. The tone employees at fancy shops used when they assumed Mihi's mom didn't speak English. The lilting, almost-laughing way some of the mean boys at school spoke, like the whole world was their very own personal inside joke.

"We inspire others to be better. If they don't have the lives they want, we inspire them to work harder," he continued. "This castle didn't just happen. Giants before me have been satisfied with castles made of brick and stone, but I reached higher. And look! I pushed the limits of what is possible with magic dust. I made history. And I did it all myself."

"He *stole* it all himself," Reese whispered.

"Too many people today are lazy. They want everything handed to them. But for those who are willing to work harder than everyone else, well"—he flashed a brilliant smile—"the future is bright."

Savannah frowned. "I don't like him."

Mihi nodded, but she couldn't look away from the suit, the hair, the sparkling white teeth. She wanted his words to be true, so, so badly.

A memory surfaced: her parents, sitting with her at the dinner table. Her mom squeezing her hand. Her dad stroking her hair.

She'd been in the Girl Scouts for a year, and when cookie season rolled around, she'd spent weeks going door-to-door, trying to sell those cookies. She'd done such a good job! She'd met so many people and sold so many boxes! She was sure she'd sold the most cookies in her whole troop, which meant she'd get the grand prize: a beautiful crown necklace, embedded with gemstones that practically looked real.

But as it turned out, she'd sold the *second least* out of everybody. Everyone else had sold boxes at their parents' offices, or had rich friends and neighbors who bought dozens of boxes.

"I can't do it," she'd told her parents. "No matter how hard I try."

And her mom had said, "You can do anything. As long as you work hard enough, you can achieve any dream."

The next week, for Mihi's birthday, her mom had surprised her with a crown necklace of her own. It wasn't as glittering as the Girl Scouts' but that didn't matter. It was even better because it was hers. And it was from her mom.

Mihi had held that memory close to her chest for

so long, and she'd played her mom's words in her head whenever something went wrong. *You can achieve any dream.*

But that mantra came with an *as long as . . .*

Those three little words had Mihi all jumbled up inside. On the one hand, it made her feel like, if she was good enough, she could do anything. On the other hand, sometimes it made her feel this out-of-control kind of fear, because what if she *wasn't* good enough?

And she didn't know how to reconcile that idea with how she saw her parents either. They worked harder than anyone she knew, and yes, they'd achieved their dream! They took care of animals and had the pet shelter they'd always wanted, and they always said Mihi and her brother were a dream come true.

But at the same time, the shelter seemed to be a constant struggle. Mihi overheard her parents late at night, fighting over bills. And she saw her mother cry when she heard how expensive Mihi's grandmother's doctor's visits were.

So . . . what if what her parents told her wasn't the whole truth? What happened if she did work hard enough, and she *was* good enough—but someone stole rain from the sky, and the world withered anyway?

This wasn't right. Her stomach turned to jagged stone, and it took Mihi a moment to recognize the feeling—one that used to be almost unfamiliar but was popping up more and more recently.

Anger.

Mihi was used to frustration and annoyance and hurt. But anger was sharper and harder and all together *wilder*, and it startled her each time she felt it.

The giant finally finished speaking. He raised his goblet once more and boomed, "To hard work!"

"To hard work!" the guests around them echoed before draining their fizzy glasses.

The music resumed. The guests began chattering and laughing again. Monsters milled about. The giant spoke to a group of werewolves, pleased as they laughed at his jokes.

Everybody seemed distracted.

But Mihi was entirely focused. "Let's find Genevieve," she said. "And then let's take this giant down."

℘ **Chapter 16** ℘

First things first: Mihi had to get into the kitchen without being noticed.

She searched for a way in until she found a waiter pushing a food cart through the party. It looked almost like a cart of dim sum—but instead of bao buns, it carried wriggling worms, tentacles oozing with black tar, and what looked like . . . *teeth.*

Mihi felt a little queasy, but she swallowed her disgust. Her parents always told her not to yuck another person's yum. Even if that yum was . . . she tried not to think about it.

Mihi pointed and whispered to her friends, "I'm gonna try to get in there." The cart was draped with a tablecloth, which meant if Mihi could duck under it, she'd be hidden.

Savannah's eyes widened. "You're gonna hide under the monster food? That's one step away from *being* monster food."

"Which is one step closer to finding Genevieve," Mihi responded.

"Wild idea," Reese said, "but not a terrible one. I'll distract the waiter. Savannah, find a way to bring the harp closer to the kitchen. Once Mihi's in there, you can play it to lure the cooks out."

Reese speed-walked over to the waiter and not-so-accidentally bumped into him. "Oh! I'm so sorry!" she exclaimed.

The waiter rushed to reassure her that everything was fine, and she began peppering him with questions.

Savannah leaned closer to Mihi. "She's so brave," she whispered as Reese asked if the tentacles were rare, medium rare, or well-done.

Mihi had to agree. Where Mihi rushed into plans, belatedly realizing the danger, Reese thought everything through. She weighed the costs and accepted the risks.

"Would you like to try one?" the waiter asked, holding up a plate. The tentacle twitched.

"Oh . . ." Reese hesitated. "Um . . ."

Mihi moved quickly. She hurried over to the cart, dodging goblins and dipping under dragon wings, and while the waiter was distracted, she slipped under the cloth. Her heart pounded.

It smelled of rotting squid and mothballs under there, and Mihi swallowed a wave of nausea. As she squeezed herself into the space, her leg cramped, and she tried not to squeak in pain. At least disguised as Genevieve, she was small enough to fit.

The cart jolted abruptly, then stopped, and Mihi nearly fell out. She struggled to rebalance.

Through the cloth, Mihi heard the waiter's muffled

voice. "I think something's wrong with this cart. It seems . . . heavier."

Mihi's pulse roared in her ears. *Panic. Panic.*

"I've heard that happens sometimes with tentacles," Reese responded. "They're very, uh, dense. Especially when the tar . . . congeals."

The waiter paused. "Really?"

"But you shouldn't tell anyone about that!" Reese added. "I used to, uh, work for the giant. And he does *not* take kindly to things going wrong."

The waiter's voice dropped to a whisper. "Thanks for the tip. Terrible guy to work for." Mihi remembered what the witch of the bizarre had said. The giant's employees didn't like him very much.

"I'll just . . . push harder," he said, and Mihi felt a simultaneous rush of sympathy for him and gratitude for Reese as the cart began to roll again.

Mihi tried to be open-minded as the waiter offered up unappetizing delicacies, but with the smell and the jerky stop-starts of the cart, she was starting to lose the battle with her nausea. Attempting to think about anything else, she strained to catch snippets of conversation.

A gravelly voice said, "This really is the most impressive castle I've ever seen."

"But a little *much*, don't you think?" said another. "Besides, I heard using dust like that wasn't even his idea."

They took a turn, and she heard, "—I promise it's a great business idea. You heard the giant. We just have to work harder—"

Another turn and: "—I spent *so* much gold on that spinning wheel, and she only fell asleep for *two hours*. Now what am I supposed to do with my life?"

Finally, she heard the swinging of a door, and the sounds and smells around her changed. Music and laughter and gossip no longer frittered around her. Instead, she heard the scrape of knives and the sizzle of frying pans.

The cart came to a stop, and slowly, quietly, oh so gently, Mihi lifted the hem of the cloth.

Peeking out, she noticed a giant-sized oven and shivered.

This was where monsters cooked children into pies. But the kitchen didn't look monstrous. It just looked *cold*, like everything else in this terrible manor.

Every surface was gleaming, polished, reflective, icy. Even the appliances seemed to be made of opaque ice, all reinforced by those wispy tendrils of mist, which seemed to be working overtime to combat the kitchen's heat.

If Mihi didn't know the dire consequences of that magic, she might've been able to appreciate the kitchen. It was beautiful, in a way. Like a kitchen from one of those home renovation shows—those big, airy, sparkling white kitchens. But Mihi could never picture actual humans cooking in them. She always imagined those kitchens smelled like bleach instead of sweet cakes, or freshly picked herbs, or warm bubbling soups.

Focus, Mihi.

She saw cooks bent over dishes and waiters rushing in and out.

But she did not see Genevieve.

Her gaze returned to the oven. What if . . . she was too late?

Without warning, her memory flashed back to the day she met Genevieve.

It was the first day of kindergarten, and Mihi remembered that bubbling nervous-excitement. She'd barely slept, and when her mom woke her that morning, she'd leapt out of bed and pulled on her pink princess outfit.

She didn't know who she'd be friends with. What if nobody liked her? What if she didn't like anybody? There was a lot to think about!

But as soon as she stepped inside her brand-new classroom—which had felt so giant-sized to her five-year-old self—she'd seen another girl, small for their age, standing wide-eyed in the corner. Her parents had already left, and she was alone.

Mihi had walked up to Genevieve and said, "Let's be friends."

And Genevieve had burst into tears. Not because she was sad or scared. But because she was *relieved*. Mihi had felt, for the first time in her life, like someone who mattered. And she'd proceeded to dry Genevieve's tears and make her smile.

As if memory had conjured her, the back door to the giant's kitchen swung open, and two waiters walked in carrying a giant piecrust on a stretcher.

There, at the center, was Genevieve, sitting cross-legged with her hands tied behind her back.

"Dessert's here," one of the waiters grunted before setting the stretcher down with a thud.

"Ex*cuse* me," Genevieve huffed. "Be gentle with me! That is so unprofessional."

Mihi tried not to roll her eyes and dropped the tablecloth before flipping her mirror open.

On one side, she saw through Savannah's mirror. On the other, she saw through Reese's.

Savannah had set hers on the ground facing her, and Mihi watched her friend drag the harp closer to the kitchen. Pure panic crossed Savannah's face as she looked at the strings.

Come on, Sav, Mihi thought, wishing she could send some confidence through the mirror.

"Hey." She heard a deep voice coming from the ballroom. "Who took the harp?"

And then another voice. "Yeah, who's that? I thought all the musicians were listed in the program!"

Savannah froze. The color fled her face.

Please, Sav. Mihi thought it even harder, as hard as she possibly could. *Do something!*

Savannah lifted her hand. It shook, as if the fear inside her was a beast she could hardly contain.

"Hey, you!" said the voice outside again. "Give that back!"

Play, Mihi thought desperately.

But Savannah sat frozen in horror, her fingertips hovering just above the strings—and the monsters were getting closer.

Chapter 17

The monsters closed in on Savannah.

She yelped. "No, wait!"

And then she strummed the harp.

A few clanging chords screeched out, and Savannah flinched. She clearly had no idea how to play. But she kept going. And as she continued, the harp glowed a soft pink.

Her shoulders relaxed, and her posture shifted. Her hands began to move differently, adeptly, coaxing gentle notes from the instrument.

Maybe this is what the fairy tale meant by a harp that played itself. It didn't *literally*, but it was magical enough that all you needed to do was strum and believe, and the music would be beautiful.

Mihi could hear it right outside. Savannah's song sounded like the soft heart-pang of waking in an unfamiliar bed on vacation—homesickness and a flash of fear, followed by the excitement of a new adventure.

Mihi's whole body ached to hear the song better, and she gripped the edge of the cart to keep from running toward it.

Thankfully, the chefs seemed to feel the same way, because she heard one of them say, "We could use a bit of a break, don't you think?"

The others murmured their agreement, and Mihi heard the door swing open again.

Through Reese's mirror, she saw all the chefs leave the kitchen and walk toward Savannah.

Which meant Mihi was in the clear. She made sure her fox mask was firmly in place and attempted to crawl out from under the cart. But in that scrunched position her leg had gone completely numb, and she tumbled out instead, rolling and landing right beneath the giant pie.

She stood up, rubbing her butt. "Ouch."

Genevieve raised a brow. "Are you a thief?"

"What?" Mihi stared at Genevieve. Her ex-friend's voice was curious and slightly amused, which was not at all how Mihi had expected her to sound. She'd *expected* Genevieve to seem a little more, you know, frightened.

"You were hiding in that catering cart like a spy— but not a very good spy. That was a very clumsy exit. And you're clearly a kid. So I assume you're trying to rob the castle."

"Genevieve, *you're* also a kid. And I'm not trying to rob anyone. Well, I guess I'm trying to rob them of their dessert. But I didn't think you'd mind that." She shot her archnemesis a pointed look, but her mask hid it.

"How do you know my name?" Genevieve tilted her head. "There's something about you that's . . . weirding me out. Take the mask off."

"We don't have time. We—"

"I absolutely demand that you take off your mask!"

How Genevieve could be so demanding just moments before her doom was a complete mystery, but Mihi was never very good at resisting her.

Sighing, she pushed the mask up onto her hair.

Genevieve's eyes bugged. She opened her mouth to scream. But before she could make a sound, Mihi reached wildly for the first thing she could find. She stuffed an apple into Genevieve's mouth.

Genevieve spit it out and gulped for air. "You're . . . *me*." She gasped.

"Temporarily. Now let's go."

Genevieve frowned. "Ew, is that what I sound like?"

Mihi counted her breaths. *One. Two. Three.*

Genevieve narrowed her eyes. "You remind me of someone. And not just me."

"I'll explain later," Mihi said. "Right now, I'm *rescuing* you. You're welcome, by the way."

"Ex*cuse* me. I'm not going to run off with a girl who looks exactly like me. You're probably a witch or an evil fairy, and while I understand wanting to look like me, I do *not* trust you."

Unfortunately, Genevieve had a point. Doppelgängers were never good news in fairy tales.

"It's me, Mihi," she explained. "Reese, Savannah, and I found your backpack by the refrigerator and followed you in. Then we took a disguise potion that got, uh, mixed up . . . You know what, that's not important right now. We have to go."

"But—but—what?" Genevieve sputtered, before adding, "That breathing thing you were doing. That *was* a total Mihi thing. Ew, Mihi, why do you *look like me?"*

Mihi took a deep breath. *One. Two*—No. She had no time for deep breaths! "Genevieve, come on!" She attempted to untie the rope around Genevieve's wrists.

But Genevieve shimmied away. "I'm waiting for someone to save me, Mihi. Go away."

"*I'm* saving you!"

Genevieve shook her head. "No. I'm thinking maybe Jack or something. He's from this fairy tale, right? That's how this whole thing works?"

Mihi gaped at her. And then she realized: Genevieve really, truly, didn't realize how much danger she was in. Which was ridiculous. She was tied up in a *pie* for goodness' sake!

But this had always been a weird thing about Genevieve. She was smart. Not Reese-level smart, but still *smart*. Except when it came to her own self-preservation. She just had this unyielding belief that everything would work out for her. Most times, it did. But in the rare cases it didn't, Genevieve was caught totally off guard. She could barely even process when things in her life went wrong.

Once, in second grade, Genevieve had slipped and landed in a pit of mud, and she'd just stared at the soil in shock, as if the earth had betrayed her.

Mihi summoned her dwindling patience. "If you want to wait around for Jack, fine. But he's not here. *We're* here. Your used-to-be friend and two *very* nice classmates. And we're trying to help you out of the situation *you* caused. But whatever."

"That can't be true." Genevieve attempted to put on her know-it-all confident act, but her voice cracked. She looked at Mihi with annoyance, like how *dare* Mihi have the nerve to shatter her fantasy?

But there was another emotion in her expression, too, a kind of plea, a flash of panic and helplessness. This, too, was a Genevieve thing. It had taken Mihi a while to notice it, but in the months before their friendship ended, she'd started to recognize Genevieve's moments of fear. As much as Genevieve pretended to—and probably *did*—look down on Mihi, whenever the world fell off-kilter, Genevieve turned to her as if Mihi were her only lifeline.

"Because . . ." she added, "because if nobody else is coming, then I'm really . . . this is really . . . scary."

Mihi returned to Genevieve's wrists. This time, Genevieve didn't protest. "Look, if you want me to leave you I will," Mihi said. "But *I* don't want to leave you. Because that would be wrong. And anyway, we need your help. The giant's been sucking rain out of the clouds to build his castle, and we want to stop him. Have you seen anything that might help?"

The knots were tight, and there were a lot of them, but Mihi was making good progress.

"He's stealing rain?" Genevieve blinked. "Well, it's not like I've been allowed to wander around the manor. But . . . I did hear him tell people to stay away from the goose room. He was *very* intense about that. And usually people only get that intense when they're hiding something valuable."

"Perfect," Mihi said, just as the final knot fell loose. "We'll start there."

Genevieve rubbed her red wrists. "You're not actually gonna *do* anything about that, are you?"

"Of course I am," Mihi said. "And you're going to help." Unfortunately, she was, in fact, a little too late.

Chapter 18

ihi slid her fox mask back over her face and beckoned for Genevieve to follow.

But just as Genevieve stepped out of the pie, the back door swung open.

A cook stared at them, two of a kind, mid-escape. They stared back. For a moment, nobody moved.

Then he opened his mouth to sound an alarm, and Mihi threw both hands up.

"Stop!" she cried.

To her surprise, he did, and Mihi blinked, trying to determine what to say. The toast she'd just heard replayed in her head—so she repeated the giant's words. "Listen," she said, heart thudding in her ears. "There is something I'd like to say."

The cook hesitated, his eyes flicking toward the ballroom.

There was, in fact, nothing Mihi wanted to say.

She was stalling, desperately and wildly—but with what? Genevieve looked at her with eyebrows raised in a way that said, *What have you gotten into now?*

The cook really could have shouted by now, but he didn't. And Mihi realized: This man worked for the giant. According to Nev, that didn't mean he *liked* the giant.

"The giant's been terrible to everyone who lives below him," Mihi said. "And I'm guessing he hasn't been very nice to his cooks either."

His lips pressed into a line, waiting for her to continue. She inhaled, exhaled, inhaled, exhaled. Inhaled. She was in over her head, and she didn't know the right thing to say, so she said how she felt.

"I don't know much about how this world works—I mean, how the world works." *Great, Mihi. Try not to tip him off that you're a Grey.* She swallowed. "But I know how it feels when people act like they're better than you. And that's not right. It's not fair. It's not fair that the giant is using the rain to make his castle nicer and bigger, instead of giving it to the people so they can *live*. And I want to change that. I have no idea how, but I have some really smart friends, and we're gonna try."

The cook paused, then gave her the slightest nod before disappearing through the back door.

He wouldn't help her. But he wouldn't stop her either.

Mihi exhaled.

Genevieve tilted her head, looking at her with something like surprise. But before either girl could say anything, the front door burst open, and all the cooks stared at them.

Mihi blinked. "Um, there is something I'd like to say?" she tried.

These cooks did not look interested.

Genevieve leaned closer to Mihi. "Yeah, I don't think that whole speech is gonna work a second time."

Perhaps if there'd been more time, Mihi would've thought of a different plan. Perhaps she would've come up with a reasonable, practical solution.

But there were also moments in life that called for quick action, and that was still something Mihi knew how to do.

The cooks moved toward the girls, leaving the front doors unguarded, and Mihi seized the opportunity. She tugged her fox mask down so it hung limply around her neck and exposed her Genevieve-face. Then she raced toward the exit and shouted, "It's me! The dessert! And I'm escaping!"

Part of Mihi's brain screamed, *BAD IDEA*. But she'd already catapulted headfirst into this haphazard plan, and there was nowhere to go but through. Her disguise spell had totally backfired, but now there were *four* Genevieves in the giant's manor. Enough, maybe, to cause a bit of confusion. And a whole lot of chaos.

Chapter 19

The cooks sprinted after her. Mihi raced through the ballroom, knocking into ghouls as she ran. Their champagne glasses shattered into ice shards as they fell to the floor.

Across the hall, Mihi saw Genevieve—the *real* one—running through the hall in a different direction. At least she finally realized she was in danger.

From elsewhere, someone called out, "There's another one!" And out of the corner of her eye, Mihi saw Reese rip the mask from her face and run the opposite way. Some of the cooks peeled off to chase her instead.

And then another cry of, "There's a fourth!"

Savannah was running too.

"The girl must be a witch!" somebody said.

The guests *oohed*. The guests *aahed*.

Running through the manor was like hurdling through a high-stakes obstacle course. Dodge a dragon here. Avoid a goblin there. Weave in and around ornate giant-sized furniture in a giant-sized living room.

Mihi could hardly breathe, and she was still so far from the exit, until she remembered: *the mask.*

Dae Ho had said the fox mask possessed some magic. An extra boost of speed and strength. She yanked it back over her face, and as soon as it was on, her legs no longer burned. She felt like she could run for miles—and fast.

With a burst of speed, she neared the exit. She just had to make it through the doors and out onto the clouds. She hoped her friends were following close behind, but she couldn't turn back to look without crashing into a villainous guest.

It helped, at least, that none of the guests tried to catch her. Some of them applauded.

"Now *this* is entertainment!" one said.

Of course they would assume her life-or-death situation was a performance for their benefit. But that worked in her favor, she supposed.

The floor rumbled, and Mihi stumbled to catch her balance.

"What is the meaning of this?" The giant's booming voice rattled Mihi's bones. "Who dares disrupt my party?"

During his speech, he'd been contained. Polite, even. Now he was full-on thunder and brimstone, the giant of nightmares. The fee-fi-foe of fairy tales.

The ground shook as his footsteps came closer, but Mihi didn't stop.

The double doors loomed in front of her, clouds and pitch-black night outside, darkness at the end of the tunnel. She just had to reach the beanstalk. She was almost there.

Then she heard Reese scream.

Mihi spun to see Reese trapped in the fist of a giant.

Savannah's scream followed as the giant plucked her up by her shirt.

"No!" Mihi cried.

Genevieve was next. A giant foot slammed down right in front of her. She ran straight into it and fell backward. He scooped her up too.

This plan had gone wrong. It had gone totally

and completely wrong. The guests began to murmur among themselves, wondering if this might not be part of the show after all. Even they looked a bit nervous.

The floor rumbled as the giant closed in, and Mihi tripped.

A shadow bore down on her and his hand loomed, blocking out the light.

Then the shadow wrapped around Mihi—and everything was dark.

Chapter 20

Mihi nearly suffocated in the humid, sweaty darkness of the giant's fist. It smelled of sweat and gasoline.

A bony elbow jabbed into her side.

"Ugh, Mihi," came Genevieve's muffled voice. "Stop squishing me."

He was holding them both in his fist.

Mihi attempted to readjust but ended up face-planting into his lifeline. If he squeezed just the slightest bit, he'd crush them, and Mihi almost expected him to—but instead, she heard a door swing open and he dropped them. She landed hard on the icy floor of a small room.

Mihi turned to see Savannah and Reese on the ground next to them, rubbing their limbs where they'd hit the floor.

"All kids look the same. But you really *are* the same," the giant growled. "Are you witches?"

Mihi hesitated. She had no idea if saying they were witches would help or hurt them, but based on the giant's guest list, she made an educated guess. "Yes?"

He narrowed his eyes. "I despise witches."

Darn.

"Your kind show no respect," he said. "But I have a party to host, and it's impolite to leave my guests waiting. I'll deal with you later."

Then he slammed the door shut, and they heard the click of a turning lock.

"Wait!" Reese shouted.

Mihi ran for the door handle, so high that she had to jump to reach it. She grabbed it and hung from it, her feet dangling above the ground. But the door handle didn't budge. Even with the fox mask's strength boost, the lock held strong.

She dropped back down and tried to catch her breath.

There were pros and cons to the situation.

Pro: The giant hadn't murdered them yet.

Con: *Yet* was a pretty important word there.

Focus, Mihi.

She took stock of the room.

The walls were made of ice. The floor was made of ice. The cold stung her nose, but a vase of fresh gardenias on the coffee table scented the room. Four luxurious velvet armchairs surrounded the table, and oil paintings of geese hung on the walls.

"This place looks . . . fancy. Like a dentist's office waiting room," she said, shuddering. It felt the same way, too, only dialed up to one hundred. Waiting for her doom, thinking about how anything was better than this, even flossing every day.

"Or like a first-class airport lounge," Genevieve said as she sank into one of the giant chairs. She didn't look at Mihi, Reese, or Savannah. She just stared off into the distance, in shock.

Mihi didn't bother rolling her eyes. Genevieve's life was very different than Mihi's, but either way, dentist's office or first-class lounge, they were trapped.

Reese paced, tapping her lips, trying to think of a plan. Savannah stood in the corner, shoulders scrunched, nervously twirling her hair. And Genevieve sat in a chair with her knees pulled to her chest, shoulders hunched, blinking fast, wearing that betrayed-by-the-world expression.

Reese and Savannah had tossed their masks off, and Mihi tugged hers back around her neck. She felt dizzy looking at three Genevieves.

In fact, she felt a little dizzy in general. She usually felt this way after a wild plan, and this one had gone considerably worse than usual. Adrenaline ping-ponged through her body. She closed her eyes. *One. Two*—

"Mihi, you made things worse," Genevieve complained.

Mihi opened her eyes. Genevieve was probably right. She'd failed to save the people of the Rainbow Realm, and she'd failed to save her former friend. The only thing she'd succeeded at was placing her friends and herself in danger as well.

But Savannah said, "No she didn't."

Savannah was still disguised as Genevieve, but Mihi was surprised by how different two identical people could look. Everything about Savannah was curled inward, like a closed fist. Her posture, her expression, the way she spoke—like she was swallowing her words to keep anyone from hearing them.

"*I* made things worse," she said. "I shouldn't have volunteered to play the harp. I just . . . seized up. My stage fright took over."

"But you *did* play," Mihi insisted. "And that distracted the cooks. You were so good."

Savannah shook her head. "I wasted too much time being scared. I thought after last time we were here I was . . . fixed. I thought I was brave now. But . . . I'm not."

"Don't beat yourself up," Reese said. "You did your best, and your best was good. We all tried our best. Well . . . mostly." She glanced at Genevieve.

Genevieve frowned. "I didn't ask any of you to save me."

"Seriously?" Mihi felt that anger boiling up inside her. She didn't like it. It was a hot, sweaty, unpleasant way to feel. But she couldn't stop it either. How could Genevieve *still* be ungrateful? "Why are you so mean to me? I've only ever tried to be your friend. I thought we *were* friends. But friends don't treat each other like this."

Genevieve's eyes widened. Her mouth fell into a little *o*. Mihi thought she wasn't going to respond at all. And then she said, very quietly, "Sorry."

Mihi blinked. Apologizing was the very least Genevieve could do. Mihi knew that. But as far as Mihi knew, this was the first time Genevieve had ever acknowledged that she'd done something wrong.

"It's hard, you know. To survive and . . . well . . ." Genevieve winced.

"Thrive," Mihi finished.

Genevieve sighed. "Yeah. But you don't care. You don't care that you're not surviving and thriving. And I don't know how you do that."

That was, perhaps, the most backhanded compliment ever.

"And you always make me feel better when I fail," Genevieve said. "Which is not often, okay?"

Mihi *did* make Genevieve feel better. That, really, was what their whole friendship was based on. And it wasn't a two-way street, because Genevieve had never done that for her. In fact, Genevieve usually made her feel *worse* for failing—or made her feel like she failed when Mihi had done nothing wrong at all!

Mihi turned to Reese and Savannah, who were frowning at Genevieve. Reese made a face at Mihi like, *Do you need backup?*

But Mihi shook her head. Despite their situation, she felt almost lighter. Because being friends with Reese and Savannah was different. Those friendships made her feel like she could exhale.

An itsy-bitsy bit of Mihi's anger at Genevieve evaporated. She didn't need to hang on to the friendship anymore. But she didn't need to hold on to the anger either.

"Okay," Mihi said.

And then the door flew open.

Chapter 21

Reese, Savannah, and Genevieve sat up as straight as, well, a beanstalk. Mihi didn't give herself a second to think. She leapt to her feet and ran for the open door.

But as she did, a giant hand tossed someone else into the room.

"I'll deal with you too," the giant said. "Unless the witches get you first."

As quickly as it had opened, the door slammed shut again.

"No!" Mihi cried.

She was so focused on the possible escape that she paid no attention to the other person until he stood and rubbed his head.

"Uh . . . whoops," he said. He was young, around

the same age as the girls, and he wore the same tattered brown clothes as Maven. His sandy blonde hair was a wild thing on top his head, desperately crying for a cut. As he pushed  some of those unruly curls out of his eyes, a shower of gold coins rained out of his shirtsleeve.

Genevieve raised her brows. "You are *definitely* a thief," she noted.

"I'm not—" the boy protested as a couple more coins dropped from his pants leg. He turned pink. "Well, can you blame me? Look how much *stuff* this guy has. The *weather*, for one thing. That's not fair."

Genevieve tilted her nose up. Disagreeing with this boy seemed to bring some of the life back to her cheeks. "Stealing is still wrong."

"Right." The boy took a step backward and cleared his throat. He tugged at an invisible thread on his sleeve, and Mihi could practically feel the nervousness radiating off him. People often felt this way around Genevieve. Mihi knew from experience.

"But what the giant's doing with the rain is theft too," Reese said, narrowing her eyes. "He just has enough power that he doesn't get punished for it."

"Exactly!" The boy looked up at Reese and grinned like she'd just gifted him a million gold coins. "Wow, that's exactly what I've been feeling, but I didn't know how to say it. And you just *said* it, like, so smartly."

Reese blinked in surprise, and Mihi could have sworn her cheeks reddened as she fought back a smile. The two stared at each other for just a second too long. Then Reese pulled back. She tugged at her Genevieve-blonde hair and looked down.

Mihi wished she could tell what Reese was thinking, but her friend was hard to read, even when she looked like Genevieve—whose expressions Mihi knew well.

Mihi took a step closer to the boy, examining him. "Are you, by any chance . . . named Jack?"

Genevieve's nose squinched with disappointment. "*This* is Jack?"

"Yeah!" He grinned. Then hesitated. Then frowned. "How did you know that? Are you actually a witch?"

Mihi held up her hands. "No. We aren't. We're—"

"Wait a minute . . ." He tilted his head, staring at them like he was putting something together. "Are you . . . *quadruplets*?"

Genevieve snorted.

"Definitely not," Reese said.

"But I understand your confusion," Savannah added.

Mihi opened her mouth to explain, but then she felt something twist and crack inside her, and her ribs turned to jelly. Spots danced before her eyes.

And she fell to the floor.

Chapter 22

Pain, pain, pain!

Mihi felt like all the bones in her body were breaking.

Well, she'd never broken a bone, but you know, this is what she *imagined* it would feel like.

Stretching, pulling, shattering, as if the universe had finally noticed they'd bent the rules of reality— and now it was enacting vengeance.

Mihi *hurt*. Becoming someone else had been relatively easy. Becoming herself, apparently, was harder.

But if the universe ripped her apart, it put her back together again. And when the pain began to ease, Mihi pushed herself back onto her feet. She rolled her wrists. She stretched her neck. She felt her face.

In the past, especially when she was with Genevieve,

Mihi wished she looked more like her friend. She'd resented her body and her round cheeks and her straight black hair that always got greasy by the end of the day.

But now that she was back to herself, back to her body, she wanted to run and shout and sing. What joy, what relief, like finally coming home. She wrapped her arms around herself.

Hadn't the witch of the bizarre said something about the power of someone being themselves?

Well, in that moment, Mihi felt powerful.

Reese and Savannah transformed quickly after her.

When they'd fully returned to themselves, they threw their arms around one another. Her *friends*. The way they truly were.

"Thank goodness," Genevieve said from her perch on the chair. She seemed entirely unfazed by the ordeal. "There's only room for one of me."

When Mihi raised her brows, Genevieve shrugged and mumbled, "Also, it's kind of nice to see you. Like, actual you."

"Oh no," Jack murmured. He seemed to be doing

his very best to flatten himself into the wall. "You *are* witches."

Mihi had kind of forgotten about him, to be honest. She sighed. "No, we just—"

"Yes, they are," Genevieve interrupted. "So you'd better do exactly as they say. Got it?"

Jack nodded vigorously.

Reese, Savannah, and Mihi exchanged a glance, but none of them bothered to correct her. If this encouraged the boy to cooperate, well . . . maybe a little white lie wasn't the *worst* thing.

"There's a witch in my village," Jack said. "She scares me."

"If you mean Maven, then yeah, she scares us too," Mihi said.

"I liked her," Genevieve said. "She's cool."

"She's one of the reasons I came," Jack continued. "People have been so hungry and so sad since the rain stopped. It's like the life is slowly draining out of them. And Maven keeps talking about how we have to *do* something. I thought if I could take some of the giant's riches, maybe I'd have enough to buy people food."

Savannah tugged her hair. "That was a brave thing to do."

Reese nodded. "We're with you. We were trying to figure out how to return the rain, before . . ." She gestured to their very fancy prison.

"I never thought there could be a way to return the rain," Jack murmured. "That's so much better than taking some gold."

"Maybe we can still try," Mihi said. "Maybe Nev's dollhouse can show us a secret passage or something."

She dug into her pockets and retrieved it, knocking the compass out in the process. It clattered to the floor, and Jack picked it up, examining it like he'd never seen anything so fascinating.

Mihi lifted the roof off the mini-manor and found the room they were currently in. Incredible. Nev had even matched the paintings. Mihi marveled at the tiny replicas.

But that was it: paintings, velvet chairs, a coffee table. And one door. No other way out. She blinked back tears.

She thought about Reese and Savannah, who would

be trapped here for the second time. She thought of the hungry people in the Rainbow Realm, whom she couldn't help. But most of all she thought of her family. What if she never saw them again?

"Um, this might be a dumb question . . ." Jack began. He shifted on his feet.

"Go on," Reese prodded.

"Uh, doesn't that symbol on the compass kind of look like this?" He pointed to the painting next to him, and Mihi blinked, her confusion snapping her back to the present moment. She didn't quite know what to say.

The symbol on her compass was a heart with a rose in the center.

That painting was a picture of geese playing poker.

She tried to figure out how to let Jack down gently.

"Those are geese," Genevieve said. "Do your eyes work?"

Savannah gasped. "Genevieve! Don't be mean."

Jack shook his head. "No, no, I don't mean the painting. I mean *this*." He pointed to the picture frame. When Mihi stepped closer, she saw a tiny carving etched into the wood.

It wasn't expertly done. In fact, it was distinctly *inexpert*, like the scratchy, scrawled carvings she found on the wooden desks at school. But he was right. It was a heart with a rose at the center.

"What are the chances?" Savannah asked as she walked up next to Mihi and ran her fingers over the carving.

"Statistically improbable," Reese responded, coming up by their side.

"Excuse me," Genevieve said. She didn't rise from her armchair, but she leaned forward. "Does anyone want to explain this whole compass thing to me?"

"I found it last time we were here, when we were at Princess Pat's castle," Mihi told her. "I don't know who gave it to me. I just found it in my dress pocket one day. But the arrow leads us to the portals home, as long as we're near one."

"And the compass was made in Maine," Reese added.

Genevieve frowned. "Like . . . the state?"

"We think so," Savannah said. "But we have no idea how it got here."

Jack cleared his throat again. "Sorry to interrupt, but what's Maine? And what does your compass have to do with this goose painting?"

Mihi ignored his first question. U.S. geography was entirely too much to explain. As for his second question, she was wondering the exact same thing. "I'm not sure."

She ran her fingers along the edges of the wooden frame, then lifted it from the wall. It was as big as she was, but relatively light. She didn't know what she'd expected to find—a secret passageway, perhaps, hidden behind the painting? A portal back home?

But there was nothing there except a thick, opaque layer of ice.

She began to put the painting back on its nail, but Reese pointed to the frame. "*Look.*"

Mihi turned the painting around to find the words *For Patricia* etched into the frame, with a small piece of metal taped next to them.

"Patricia," Savannah said. "Like the princess?"

Reese frowned. "Or like the person the princess named herself after. The person Bertha knew . . ."

The mystery of it itched at Mihi's mind, but she didn't have much time to consider it, because she was too busy inspecting the metal object. "Oh my," she whispered.

"What is it?" Genevieve asked. Giving up all pretense of not caring, she finally abandoned the armchair and rose on her tiptoes behind them, trying to see over Savannah's shoulder.

Mihi pried it off the frame and ran her fingers over the metal. She could hardly believe it. "It's a key."

Chapter 23

Savannah was the tallest, so she was the only one who could reach the doorknob without jumping. She held the key above her head and pushed it into the lock. It fit perfectly.

Mihi, Reese, Genevieve, and Jack crowded around her, watching as she turned the key. Mihi silently begged, *Work, please work. Set us free.*

The tiniest *click* echoed from inside the lock—and the door swung open. Mihi's breath rushed out. Every nerve in her body danced a jig. She fought the urge to sprint out of their prison.

Jack stepped forward, ready to walk right through, but Reese pulled him back and shut the door again. "We can't just waltz out. We need a plan."

Jack's eyes widened. "I didn't even think of that. Good idea."

Genevieve smiled sweetly, like she always did before a sharp-tongued barb. "Will this plan be better than your plan to rescue me?"

Savannah frowned. "You were about to be baked into a pie. This is better than *that*."

Genevieve seemed to remember that and sighed. "Fine."

Reese turned to Mihi. "Is she always like this?"

"Kinda," Mihi said, but she wasn't so bothered anymore. She lifted the top of the miniature wooden manor again. Right now, they appeared to be in a back corner of the manor. The kitchen, dining room, and ballroom were in front of them. "We can't go out the way we came, but it seems like there's a way out the back, and the route is quick. It's almost a straight line from here to the back door."

"Is that mini-castle magic too?" Jack asked.

"It's made from a special kind of wood that—" Reese hesitated, surely trying to find a more logical explanation. She gave up. "Yeah, basically."

Jack grinned. "Awesome."

Reese bit back a smile before growing serious. "The giant currently believes we're trapped, so he won't be on the lookout. That's a huge point in our favor."

"So let's escape," Genevieve said. "Why are we all standing around?"

"Well . . ." Mihi pointed to a nearby room in the miniature manor, what looked like a large hallway lined with tiny wooden geese. "This looks like the goose room. And remember when you said he's probably hiding something valuable there?"

"Hey wait." Jack pointed to a room right off the goose hall. "Does that room look like a heart to you?"

Mihi tilted her head. It did, in fact, look like a heart. "Yes, but we should focus—"

"I heard people in my village talking about how the giant trapped the rain in his heart. Which I thought was kinda weird. I thought it was . . ." He paused. "What's the word for a phrase you use to describe a feeling, but it's not actually real, it's . . ."

"A metaphor," Reese supplied.

"Yeah! That!" He grinned. Then his grin faded. "But I guess it wasn't a metaphor, because it's real."

Mihi tried to keep her voice down. She always got

louder when she got excited. "Jack's and Genevieve's stories both line up. Of course the giant told people to avoid the goose room, because that's where he keeps the stolen rain."

Reese nodded, and Mihi could tell that she, too, was trying not to get excited. "And if we can get into that heart-shaped room, maybe we can figure all this out."

Mihi grinned. "We can save everyone!"

"That's brilliant!" Jack said.

Savannah bit her lip, considering, until Genevieve piped up. "That sounds unnecessarily dangerous," she said.

The heart-shaped room was still in the general direction of the exit, but that path would probably take twice as long. Every extra second they spent here was dangerous—and who knew what waited for them in those rooms?

"We've taken dangerous detours before . . ." Mihi said.

"And we survived," Reese finished.

Savannah took a deep breath before saying, "It's worth a try."

"I can't believe you're gonna help me and my village!" Jack said. "Witches are the *best*."

"Ex*cuse* me." Genevieve folded her arms over her chest. "Don't I get a vote?"

"Genevieve," Mihi said softly, "think of how many people we could help."

"Oh, come on, this is a fairy tale. They aren't real people."

Jack shifted back and forth on his feet, looking uncomfortable. "Um. I mean . . . we are."

Mihi frowned. "Just because they're from a different world doesn't mean they don't matter."

Genevieve uncrossed her arms, and her expression softened, but she still shook her head. "It's not worth putting ourselves in danger."

Savannah spoke up. "I'm afraid too. But we put ourselves in danger last time we were here, and it was worth it. We survived, and we helped the princess, and we helped change her kingdom for the better."

"We're pretty good at this helping thing," Mihi added.

"I'm not *afraid*," Genevieve protested, but her

voice wobbled. "I just really, really don't want to be here anymore. I want to go home."

"Me too," Jack said softly. "And my home won't survive without the rain."

"If we want any chance of success, we should go now," Reese said. "The giant said he'd come back, and I don't want to be here when he does."

"Agreed," Mihi said. To Genevieve she added, "Come on. We'll show you what it feels like to change the world."

Chapter 24

The five kids crept through the manor, careful not to make a sound, leaning into shadows wherever they could.

The girls knew themselves, and they knew their power. *They* had become the dangerous creatures lurking in the dark—the creatures who could take down a giant.

When they made it to the door of the goose hall, Mihi braced herself. "I'll lead the way," she whispered, wrapping her hand around the knob. It turned in her palm, and she held her breath as it *creak-creak-creaked* open. The sound echoed off the icy walls, fear amplifying the volume.

But the kids were in the clear. Everyone was partying at the front of the manor, so the back of the manor was empty.

Mihi stepped inside.

The first thing that hit her was the smell—hay and feathers. The unmistakable, oh-so-familiar scent of a birdcage.

And then she saw the geese, hundreds of them. Each goose had their own bed made of hay and leaves and dirt, and they all slept with their heads and necks tucked under their wings.

Their feathers were soft and fluttery and golden, and Mihi wondered if she'd heard the fairy tale wrong, or maybe she'd just misinterpreted. Maybe these weren't geese that laid golden eggs. Maybe they were just . . . golden geese.

And judging by the goose art everywhere in the manor, maybe the giant just really loved geese.

That made the giant seem a little less evil to Mihi. Which was . . . unsettling. If he wasn't simply an evil monster, if he was capable of treating other living creatures kindly, then how could he hurt all the people beneath him without a second thought? Did he forget those people mattered too? Or did a bigger, cooler castle just matter more?

That was its own kind of villainy, to wall yourself

so far off from other people that you forgot to care. Mihi shuddered. The thought made the ice castle feel a few degrees colder.

"Be very quiet," she whispered. "Geese are loud, so we don't want to wake them."

They tiptoed past the birds, making their way toward the giant's heart.

The room was completely silent aside from the occasional goose coo and rustle of feathers, and by the time they'd made it halfway across the goose chambers, Mihi began to feel that hopeful flutter. They could return the rain to the people. They could *do* this.

And then she heard it: a *tap-tap, tap-tap, tap-tap.* She froze. *Footsteps.*

Someone was following them.

Chapter 25

These light, barely there footsteps clearly didn't belong to a giant, so who was it? One of the monsters from the party?

Mihi turned, heart seizing—until she saw . . .

A goose.

Unlike the rest of the geese, this one wasn't golden. This one's feathers were grey and molting. It was bald in some places, and it walked with a bit of a limp. Altogether, it was rather unfortunate-looking.

And Mihi loved it instantly.

It looked up at Mihi and cooed.

"It's about to attack!" Jack whisper-hissed.

But Mihi shook her head. She knew animals. She squatted and held out her hand, and the goose nudged its head against her palm.

Her heart melted. "Aren't you so sweet?"

Genevieve scrunched her nose. "Something's wrong with that one."

"Nothing's wrong with it," Mihi said.

"Do your parents have geese at their pet shelter?" Reese asked.

Mihi shook her head. "We get birds sometimes when their owners surrender them or when someone finds an injured bird on the sidewalk. But I always thought geese were scary. I guess I misjudged them."

"They *are* scary," Savannah said.

"They can be," Mihi said. "But only when they're defending their families or their territory."

Genevieve cleared her throat. "That's nice, but shouldn't we be saving that town or whatever?"

She was right. Mihi gave the goose one last pet. "Bye now," she said.

She stood to leave, and the goose waddled closer, nuzzling her ankles.

Mihi hesitated. "Go away," she said.

"*Herr-onk,*" the goose responded.

The goose *was* loud. Mihi winced and listened for

footsteps, but nobody came running. The other geese went on sleeping.

She turned and began walking. The goose followed.

"No, Goose, I mean it," Mihi whispered. "Stay."

They turned to walk away. The goose followed.

"This is not good," Savannah said.

Jack thought for a moment, and then, as if he'd had the most brilliant idea, he said, "Why don't we *steal* the goose?"

Reese raised her brows. "Because that leads to us being chased by an angry giant."

"She's right. Trust us on that one," Mihi said. She took a few steps toward the heart-shaped room. They were almost out of the goose chamber. When the goose followed, she told it sternly, "It's been very nice to meet you. But you can't come with us."

The goose decided that it very much *could* come with them. It waddled closer.

Genevieve sighed. "Mihi, you can't reason with a goose. You have to scare it away." She stood between Mihi and the bird and flapped her arms in an attempt to be threatening. "Now, *shoo!*"

The goose raised its wings, flapping back at Genevieve before it opened its beak. "HERRRR-ONK!"

Mihi watched as if in slow motion as all the other birds began to wake. They flapped their wings. They opened their beaks.

HERR-ONK, HERR-ONK, HERRRRR-ONK.

The sound was deafening.

The five kids looked at one another, eyes wide. Hundreds of honking geese were loud enough to wake this entire realm. The rest of the manor would surely hear.

"What do we do?" Genevieve squeaked.

Mihi could only think of one option. "Run."

Chapter 26

They burst into the heart-shaped room—and Mihi gasped. Filling the room was a giant contraption made of tubes and wires and metal. One tube ran straight through a hole in the ground, and Mihi could see it beneath them, sucking water right out of the clouds. Magic dust floated around the contraption, tickling Mihi's nostrils.

"He really is stealing it," Jack murmured. "I knew it, but it's different to actually *see* it."

Reese pushed her glasses up her nose as she surveyed the contraption. "Fascinating."

"We have to get out of here," Genevieve said.

"Just give Reese a few minutes," Mihi told her. "She can figure it out."

"Maybe," Reese amended.

Genevieve gaped at them. "A few minutes? Have you lost your *minds*? We're going to *die*."

"We are, uh, not going to die," Savannah said uncertainly.

Mihi locked the door and pointed to a thick ice table beside them. "While Reese works, let's barricade the door."

Jack and Savannah rushed to help, and the three of them pushed all their weight against the table. Genevieve hesitated, but when she heard thundering footsteps outside, she hurried into position.

They pushed. It moved slowly, inch by minuscule inch.

"I've heard stories online of people showing amazing strength in life-or-death situations." Mihi grunted. "One time, I read about a mom who lifted an entire car in the air to save her baby."

"Helpful fact, Mihi," Genevieve deadpanned.

The footsteps grew closer.

"Mihi!" Savannah exclaimed. "Your mask."

"Oh yeah!" In all the chaos, she'd forgotten the fox mask, still dangling around her neck. She pulled it up over her face and shoved.

With the extra boost of strength, the table slid into position—just as the giant rattled the knob.

"Let me in!" he roared from behind the thick ice block of a door. It shook as he pounded his fist.

"Reese!" Mihi shouted. "Hurry!"

"I'm trying! Just a few more seconds!"

"We don't have a few seconds!"

Reese rearranged the tubes. The pounding grew louder.

"I don't know, I don't know, I don't know," Reese stammered, her words running together. "I don't understand. I'm not smart enough—"

Mihi interrupted her panic. "You're the smartest person I know."

"You can do it, Reese!" Jack said with utmost confidence.

"We believe in you!" Savannah added.

A crack formed in the ice door.

Mihi *did* believe in Reese. She believed, 100 percent, that Reese could figure this out. But maybe not in the next second. They were out of time.

"Reese!" Genevieve shouted. "It's just capillary action, remember? Like our science fair project. You won it for us. It was all you."

Reese blinked at Genevieve for a second, shocked. Then she nodded once, turned back to the contraption, and got to work.

Her hands flew, twisting wires, moving tubes. The crack in the door grew.

"Almost there!" Reese said.

The door shattered into pieces.

"I did it!" Reese cried.

"Take cover!" Mihi screamed.

The kids dove for cover just as the ice table flew back and exploded against the wall.

The giant stood in front of them, surrounded by a horde of monsters.

It was too late. They were cornered.

The ground shook beneath them, and Mihi gritted her teeth, waiting for her doom. But it didn't come.

It took her a second to realize that this time, the earthquake wasn't coming from giant footsteps, because the giant was standing right in front of them.

Which meant . . .

The floor beneath Mihi grew slippery. She heard a quiet *drip*. And then came the sound of thunder.

Chapter 27

The giant's castle wasn't melting quickly. But it *was* melting. It was big and strong enough to stand a while longer, but it was so very close to the sun. Without a constant stream of reinforcing rain to keep the ice cold, how many hot days could it last?

The sound of water rushed beneath them.

And it was as if, all at once, everyone recovered from the shock.

"*Rain,*" Jack said.

"*Rain?!*" The giant roared. He lunged for them, his face twisting into ugly hate. The kids dodged, but barely.

They were trapped. How long could *they* last?

The giant lunged again, and the only thing that saved

them was the giant slipping on the melting floor. He slid, whizzing just past them.

"DO SOMETHING," he shouted to his guests, but they exchanged glances behind his back. Nobody seemed to want to get their hands dirty. Or their party clothes wet.

"We actually should be goin—" one of them attempted, but the giant's roar cut them off.

He grasped for Savannah, who dodged, slamming hard into the wall.

And Mihi had a wild idea.

They were trapped. There was only one way out.

Unless, of course, they made another.

On the other side of the room, the exploding table had left some chips in the wall, and now that weakened area was melting slightly faster. "Over here!" she shouted.

She ran-slipped-slid over to the contraption and stood directly in front of it. It was the second time tonight that she'd called attention to her escape.

Best not to make a habit of that.

The giant turned to her and ran-slipped-slid in her direction.

Closer, closer.

Mihi ducked at the last possible second, squeezing her eyes shut, and then—*crash*.

The giant went slamming into his own contraption, destroying it beyond repair—and then kept skidding toward the damaged wall until he burst through, out onto the clouds.

The kids didn't waste any time. They leapt out through the giant-sized hole, and they ran.

Chapter 28

"To the beanstalk!" Mihi cried as the giant pushed himself to his feet.

Behind them, they heard him growl, "You. Will. *Pay for this.*"

He stumbled after them, tie ripped, hair disheveled, pants leg torn.

They sprinted, but even in his injured state, he was bigger and faster. He leapt onto a cloud in front of them and blocked their path.

"Please," Mihi begged. "Let us go home."

"We haven't stolen anything," Genevieve added.

"You've stolen *everything!*" The giant boomed.

Mihi knew she should grovel. If they wanted any chance of survival, she should apologize. And she *was* sorry. She was sorry to her friends. She was sorry to have put them in this position.

But she wasn't sorry about the rain.

People like the giant—the strongest, the richest, the biggest—stole important things from others. That was the way things were.

But that wasn't how they always had to be. Anything was possible. After all, magic was real.

"The rain never belonged to you," she said.

Anger flashed in the giant's eyes. "It *all* belongs to me. I worked for it. I figured it out. I dedicated my whole life to advancing our understanding of dust magic."

Before Mihi could respond, she heard the flutter of feathers, and the little grey goose waddled up and stood in front of her, as if to protect her.

"No, go back!" Mihi whispered, trying to shoo it away.

"You'll get hurt, little one," Savannah added, voice trembling.

But the bird refused to listen. It stepped in front of Mihi and her friends and opened its beak. It spread its wings. It *HERR-ONKED*.

The giant completely ignored it as he closed in.

"Thanks, Goose, but you can't help us now," Mihi murmured.

The giant's lips twisted into a mocking smile, and Mihi wrapped her arms around herself.

But the goose wasn't done. It fluttered its wings . . . and began to grow. It grew and grew—until it was even bigger than the giant.

The goose hissed at the giant, spreading its wings to protect the kids.

"That goose is huge!" Genevieve screamed, as if they hadn't noticed.

Mihi stared in shock and awe. "It's defending its territory."

"Or its family," Savannah murmured.

The giant stared at the goose with a mixture of confusion, horror, and hurt. "You're not supposed to turn on me. I—I treated you all so well."

He attempted to step around the goose, but it blocked his path.

He narrowed his eyes. "If you want to play it that way, then fine. Good luck." He tossed a handful of dust at the kids, and they stumbled as their cloud reverberated.

The mist beneath their feet disintegrated.

And they began to fall.

Chapter 29

If things had gone differently, Mihi might have
landed on the twisting branches of the Treehouse
Village. Or in a patch of briar thorns. Or she might
have kept falling and falling forever.

Fairy tales often had tragic, gruesome endings.

But instead, she landed on feathers. Grey, molting
feathers, with a few bald patches.

"Goose!" she cried.

The newly giant goose carried Mihi and her friends
gently through the rainy night, down to the world
below.

"This was a weird day," Genevieve said, crinkling
her nose at the bird's rather pungent scent.

Mihi couldn't help but laugh at the understate-
ment. "Welcome to the Rainbow Realm."

"It's always exciting," Savannah said. "In a terrible kind of way."

"But we're going home now, right?" Genevieve asked.

Mihi, Reese, and Savannah nodded vigorously.

Jack frowned. "Wait . . . what do you mean going home?"

"We're not actually witches," Reese explained. "We're Greys."

"Whoa." He paused, and Mihi wondered if he'd be afraid or disgusted, like some of the others they'd met in this world. Not everybody liked outsiders. But he just grinned and said, "That's even cooler."

The goose landed softly on the muddy ground, right at the base of the beanstalk. The kids slid off its back, and Mihi reached up to pet its wing.

"Thank you," she said.

Pleased, it ruffled its feathers and proceeded to shrink to normal goose size.

In the trees above them, they heard shouts, and Mihi looked up to realize the people of the Treehouse Village had come outside. They tilted their heads to the sky, laughing and marveling at the rain.

The only person who looked down at them was an older woman, with sandy blonde hair. "Jack!" she cried.

Jack grinned. "I should get back to my mom," he said to the girls. "I have a feeling it's gonna be a good night here in our village."

"Good night, Jack," Mihi said. "Don't climb any more beanstalks."

He laughed. "I won't. It was really cool to meet you four. You're all, like, really good at stuff."

His gaze lingered for an extra fraction of a second on Reese, until they both looked away, embarrassed.

"I'm sorry we didn't get you a golden goose or a magical harp," she told him.

His eyes widened. "Why are you apologizing? You gave us back the rain!"

He looked up at the sky, grinning even wider as raindrops slid over his face, washing away the dirt. Then he waved and took off toward his home.

"We should go too," Mihi said, pulling the candies out of her pocket and leading the girls toward Maven's tree. To Genevieve, she explained, "As soon as we eat these, a portal home will appear at the base of the tree."

She handed everyone a candy, and Genevieve popped hers right into her mouth. "See ya," she said as the portal appeared, and then she disappeared through it without waiting for the rest of them.

Reese sighed. "Wow."

"Wow is right," Savannah said, shaking her head.

Mihi just shrugged. She was glad they'd saved Genevieve . . . but it was a relief to get a final moment in the realm without her.

She knelt beside the goose. "Take care of yourself when I'm gone, okay?"

The goose honked before nuzzling its head against her palm.

From up above them, someone drawled, "Well, look who got themselves a new pet. How very quaint."

Mihi looked up to see Maven, hopping between branches and lowering herself to the ground next to them. "You three did well."

"The rain was tricky to figure out," Reese said. "But not too tricky for me."

Maven glanced at the sky, as if she'd forgotten it was raining. "Oh, yes, the rain is obviously very nice. But I meant thanks for gathering me all that intel."

Mihi frowned. "What?"

Maven pulled a compact mirror from her tattered dress—one that matched the three she'd given Reese, Mihi, and Savannah. "I got to learn a lot about the most villainous creatures in the land."

"You have one of those too?" Savannah asked.

"Of course," Maven said. "You didn't think I'd give you some of my magic without having a way to spy on you, did you? How naive."

Reese narrowed her eyes. "We should've listened to Jonathan. He knew we shouldn't trust those mirrors."

"Those mice should really stop meddling," Maven said. "And I'll take this as my payment." The miniature manor zapped from Mihi's pocket, snapping into

Maven's palm. Mihi stared. Before now, Maven hadn't shown any magical ability beyond her mirrors.

"Your payment?" Savannah asked.

"I'm the one who helped you four get into the giant's manor in the first place."

"You helped us get *in*," Reese said. "But *we* got ourselves out. We don't owe you anything."

"Clever girl. But if you were *really* clever, you'd know that it's not about what the poor owe. It's about what the powerful can take."

"You sound just like the giant," Mihi said, with horror.

Maven just laughed. A sound like ice.

"That wooden dollhouse won't be useful to you anymore, anyway," Reese said. "I think the manor is melting. It won't look like that forever."

"Oh, sweet little Reese. You really don't understand magic, do you?"

Reese bristled.

"Greys are always underestimating how much power magical items hold." Maven tossed the dollhouse back and forth between her hands, taunting the girls. "You did the same thing with that apple in the Healing Orchard. Don't you know how much power a magic apple holds?"

If Mihi had any doubt that Maven would one day be the evil queen, she didn't anymore. "What are you planning to do with the dollhouse?" she asked. "Didn't you already get what you wanted?"

"Magic is scarce in this world, little Greys, and the person who holds the most magic holds the most power." Maven's eyes glinted. "The giant is just the beginning. There are forces far more powerful in this realm. And I promise you: One day, I'll be one of them."

And without waiting for a response, she opened her compact mirror, vanishing into a portal of her own.

The girls were silent for a while.

"We shouldn't have trusted her," Mihi said finally.

"And yet, we didn't have another choice," Reese said, placing a hand on Mihi's back. "Let's not worry about this for now. Let's go home."

Mihi nodded, though she felt shaken.

When she heard yet another voice behind them,

Mihi thought for a moment it was Maven, coming back to say, *Just kidding; sorry that was so weird!*

But then she caught the scent of toothpaste.

"There you are," said a familiar voice, prim and humorless as always. "I was hoping to catch you before you left."

The girls turned to see a woman, with her grey hair pulled into a tight bun. Her thin lips stretched into a tighter line.

A woman who, once upon a time, tried to have them *disposed of*.

The name fell out of Mihi's mouth, thick with anger. "*Bertha.*"

Chapter 30

"Oh, come on," Reese said. "We've been through enough today."

"And we're about to go home," Savannah added. "Please let us leave."

Bertha sighed. "I know you girls don't like me, but we don't have time for this."

"No, we don't," Mihi said, linking her arms through Reese's and Savannah's and turning toward the portal. She unwrapped her candy.

"Wait!" Bertha said. It was the first time she'd ever sounded . . . less than put together. She sounded *panicked*. "I'm not the bad guy. I want to send you home. Really, I do. But . . . it's the princess."

Mihi's heart stopped. Slowly, she turned back to Bertha. "What happened?"

"She's gone. And I need . . . I need your help to find her."

"Of course we'll help find her," Savannah said, with a conviction that surprised Mihi. Mihi knew Savannah would want to help Pat, of course. But she hadn't expected her to say it so quickly.

Mihi nodded. "Definitely."

Reese's brows pinched. "Why do you need us?"

"Because someone needs to take the train between worlds," she said. "And you might be the only people who can do it."

Reese, Mihi, and Savannah exchanged a glance. The *Station*—and the realms that lay beyond it.

"You'll need to collect some things from the Grey World too. It will be a difficult journey."

Savannah's eyes widened. "But if we go back to our world, who knows how much time will pass before we're back."

"My watch," Reese said. She lifted her wrist with the magical wooden watch. "The witch of the bizarre said I could use it to link time between worlds. We can go back, get what we need, and return without too much time passing."

"How did she know we'd need that?" Mihi whispered. The witch had said she knew everything. Perhaps she knew the future.

"What happened to Pat?" Savannah asked Bertha. "Where did she go?"

"She's worried about our realm. It seems the giant wasn't our only threat. And though we now have rain, our world is still fading." Bertha pressed her thin lips into a line. The wrinkles around her face deepened, like a map to her past, to all the secrets she kept. "The princess believes that if she takes enough magic from the other realms, she can save our own."

"Can she?" Mihi asked.

"Perhaps," Bertha said through gritted teeth, as if she were forcing the word out. "But she has no idea what lies beyond the dragon trains. There's great magic and great danger, and the princess will not survive it on her own."

Mihi shivered. "So how do we help her?"

"Each of you must gather something from your world. An item that evokes a memory," Bertha explained. "Gather the items as quickly as you can.

Then meet me back here, and I will prepare you for your journey."

Bertha appeared to be telling the truth, but they knew they couldn't trust her. What if this was another trap? They'd already fallen for Maven's.

But then again . . . Pat was in danger. And what if they were the only ones who could help?

"Are you in?" Mihi asked her friends.

Reese raised a brow. "Do you still need to ask? Of course."

"Of course," Savannah echoed.

Of course. The princess needed them. There were other realms to explore. And adventure awaited.

Credits

EDITORIAL

Melissa Zar . . . . *Marketing*
Mary Van Akin . . . . *School & Library Marketing*
Chantal Gersh . . . . *Publicity*
Molly Ellis . . . . *Publicity*
Jen Edwards . . . . *Sales*

REPRESENTATION

Faye Bender . . . . *Literary Agent*
Jasmine Lake. . . . . *Film Agent*